STRAIGHT TO THE POINT BOOKS
P R E S E N T S

A Twisted Tale of Fate and Faith!

BLACK-OUT ON BANKHEAD

a novel

By

Antoinette Smith

STTP Books
Riverdale, GA

Published in the U.S.A. by
Straight to the Point Books
Riverdale, Georgia

Copyright © 2013 by Antoinette Smith

ISBN: 1-930231-53-9 / 978-1-930231-53-5

Editor: Windy Goodloe
Cover Design: Marion Designs
Interior Book Layout: The Rod Hollimon Company

Printed in the United States of America

Acknowledgements

I would like to, first and foremost, thank God for giving me the ability to write. Not only did He give me a gift and a talent, He also gave me the strength to speak up about my past and help others in pain as well. I strongly believe that God has a purpose for everyone's life.

I have to thank my Dream Team— Mr. Rod Hollimon, my publisher/friend; Ms. Windy Goodloe, my excellent editor/friend; and Mr. Keith Saunders, book cover designer.

I have to give thanks to my God-Mommy (Myola Smith) and my God-Daddy (Mr. Dennis Pete). I want to thank you two for the never-ending motivation that you give me and the unconditional love that I feel from you guys.

I would like to thank my fans for believing in me. I would like to also thank my fans for keeping me lifted, by letting me know that they are indeed looking forward to my next book.

I would like to give a special thanks to Ocean's 66 in College Park, Big Daddy's Catering, Wheels and Tires by Johnnie Bailey.

I would also like to give a special thanks to my Mexican family at El Ranchero Mexican restaurant in College Park. I will list all of their names because they are all very special to me, so here goes... George, Robert, Nacho, Penguin, Cheo, Alicia, Luis, Juan Luis, Crilin, Chava, Elias a.k.a Fred Flintstone, Sulvador, Memo, Joaquin, Cesar, Gus, Paco, El Jaliskillo, Antonio a.k.a Harry Potter, Jackie Chan, Nasa, That Red Bitch, Tifany, a.k.a Girl Power, Daniel, Christian, Danielle & Maria (we miss you),Beto, Chunga, Negro, Miguel, Chuto, Wicho, Hugo, Tito, Zorro, Gilles Saint-Germain, and Cacheton.

I would also like to thank Blue and his Dark Blue Security Team— Rico_Strong, Tee, Cedric Williams, and Tawan.

I would also like to thank the College Park Police Department.

I can't forget to give a special thanks to my baby Dee!!"

I have to say…if it wasn't for pain, I wouldn't be who I am today. Sometimes pain is good, so don't look at it as a bad thing.

To my kids, who are known as my 5 Lights, I write for you, for us— Pinky! Driah! Clyde! Chicken! Fat Boy!

I meant it when I said that I would write us out of the hood… I love you all so much!

I would like to also thank Lupe and his crew at El Nopal Mexican Restaurant

You Only Need One Person to Believe in You and That's You!

Antoinette Smith

A Special Dedication

To My Loved Ones and Friends Who are Gone Too Soon and Most Definitely Never Forgotten...

Hattie Lee Reid Pearson

Oscar Pearson

Vurilyn Toon

Harry Pearson

Willie Pearson

Lucile Brown

Arthur Brown

Nelson "Hump" Redmon

Tremeesa "Rat" West

Yvonne "Sister" Walker

Claudette McGhee

Willie McGhee

Patricia Ann Walker

Sabrina "Shawn" Murphy

Carrie Mae Wilson

Kathy "Kitty Kat" Carter

Daryl Carter

Acie "Hubbard" Wilson

Pearline Strowder

Catherine "Dot Dee" Simpson

Robin Lynn Jones

Devorris "DMoss" Moss

Beth Nicole "Candygurl" Dodson

Omar "O" Jerrod Brown

Ronald Jerome Holston

Michael Jackson

Whitney Elizabeth "Nippy" Houston

Trayvon Martin

Ms. Jeanette Wright

Annette Jones

Willie Frank Webb, Jr

Trevion Davis

Mr. Kwik

God picks special flowers,
and these are a few that He added to His Heavenly Garden.

From the Twisted Mind of a Gemini

Growing up in the hood was never fun,
Especially when I had to protect myself from a gun.
It didn't matter what time of the day it was. The bullets would always fly
And on my bedroom floor is where my body would lie.
I didn't even have time to cry,
And, when I did go outdoors, I would have my head held up high.
"It's not where you live. It's how you live," they say,
But it didn't matter because my granny always made a way.
She was a praying grandmother.
Even though I never had my real mother,
I thought that once I became grown my life would be peaches and cream,
But I was only fooling myself and had to wake up from that dream.
I thought that I was ready for the streets because I was tough,
But they were always cold, mean, and always rough.
I had to do something and think of it quick
Because being broke was only making me sick.
I didn't want God to think that the devil would win
Because getting money by any means was my biggest sin!

Chapter 1: *The Hood*

As far as I can remember, I've always been called by my nickname — Black. It wasn't because of my skin complexion; it was because of my curly, jet black, silky hair. And I always kept it cut in a low fade with deep waves. I was dark skinned, tall, and slim.

My granny gave me that nickname when I was about three years old. She said I looked like a black Cuban because my hair was wavy, and she kept it in a ponytail. But she cut it when I was in the fifth grade. She, also, told me that, often times, I was mistaken for a little girl. But there ain't shit girlie about me. I am a one hundred percent thoroughbred nigga.

I was the only child, and I lived in the projects on Bankhead. They were known as the Bricks, and I have witnessed more than any seventeen-year-old boy should have to see. I lived with my granny and my alcoholic-ass Uncle Red.

Granny was my mother and my father because both of my parents were dope fiends, and I didn't care to be around them too much. My granny was up in age, and we were living on her fixed income. It wasn't much, but we managed, and I respected her so much for that. She was such a strong woman to me. I loved my granny so much, and, as long as we had a roof and a floor, that was pretty much all that mattered.

We had a two bedroom apartment. I had to share a room with Uncle Red. We didn't have everything I wanted coming up, but she made sure I had a hot meal and clothes on my back. I mean, she cooked a good, slow cooked soul meal every day, and I didn't miss a meal. I didn't wear the most stylish clothes and shoes. I had to wear Wrangler and Rustler jeans and Macgregor tennis shoes.

My granny always said, "Boy, the clothes don't make you; you make the clothes."

But you couldn't tell my classmates that because they would tease me and crack jokes on me all the time. Growing up in the hood on the Westside was trouble bound. I was never looking for trouble, but, somehow, it would always seem to find me. Trouble was practically my middle name. Trouble would always find me, especially in high school. I was always finding myself in the principal's office for fracturing a couple of jaws. I got tired of my classmates cracking jokes on me about my unfashionable wear. My teacher Mr. James would often say, "Kill them with kindness."

He would tell me things like "You are an A student, and your future is bright". I wasn't trying to hear that shit as I sat in class in a tight-ass turtleneck and in a pair of Uncle Red's nut huggers. I was so mad and really wanted to kill one of them for clowning on me in front of Kimmy.

Kimmy was a girl who lived in the 3500 section of the Bricks, and I lived in the 2500 section. She was only a street over, and I would often see her taking a shower from my bedroom window. She was so pretty to me. Her eyes were hazel, and I could picture myself sliding ice on her pecan body. Those hazel eyes weren't hers, but she would say, "If my mama bought them, then they are mine." She always wore her hair in a mushroom, and she looked like Stacey Dash. And I would lie in my bed and jack my dick to their sexiness.

Kimmy was my ideal choice for a girlfriend, too, because she was so smart. She passed every pop quiz and every test that Mr. James gave. She lived with her mama, and her mama didn't play that hot tail girl shit. She made sure that Kimmy didn't sleep around.

In the Bricks, kids were either being raised by their strung out parents or their grandparents. It was just like that. We were all low income families looking for a way out. And half of our parents were weak because they had turned to drugs, instead of a better life. My mama was one of them who had fallen weak for the crack. It wasn't a secret that she was on drugs because she would come around and steal Granny's bill money. I never understood how she could take from her own mama. But, hey, some people take their own mama's lives.

Priscilla was her name, and I called her by her first name because she didn't deserve to be called *Mama*. Kimmy's mama was strong, though. She wanted to get out of the hood. She worked at a warehouse on Fulton Industrial Boulevard. And she had a car. It was rare to see someone in the hood with a car.

****

I looked over at Kimmy in class as Mr. James stood there in my face, grilling me. *Fuck killing them with kindness,* I thought. School really bored the shit out of me, and I didn't see the point. I knew how to add and read, and that was all I would need in the real world. I wanted to grow up and be like Ray Ray and Peanut.

They were cousins, and they sold drugs in our hood. They had the most stylish clothes, and they had cars with the big shiny rims. *I am going to be just like them,* I thought as I cracked a smile and rubbed my chin.

Then, all of a sudden, Mr. James screamed, "Mr. Demetrius Terrell Smith!"

I ignored him and looked around at the class as if he wasn't talking to me. Then, I looked at him, and said, "My name is Black."

The whole class laughed, but Mr. James didn't see shit funny. I looked over at Kimmy, and I could see that she had a sense of fear for me on her face.

The bell rang, and Mr. James said, "Everyone is excused but Mr. Black."

I was pissed because Kimmy and I usually walked home together. I sat at my desk and watched Kimmy's sexy ass leave class. I knew she wasn't going to wait for me because her mama timed her and always waited on their porch for her to come home.

I looked at Mr. James as he shut the door and looked over at me and said, "Now, what seems to be the problem? Why do you have to disrupt my classroom?"

"Why do the kids have to tease me and talk about my clothes?" I asked.

"Listen to me, son. You're not in school for a fashion show. You are here to get your education and become a successful black man in the real world. Because, after school, this is it. Your granny will not be able to save you and come to your rescue. How is your granny anyway?"

"She's making it."

"Well, it's bad enough that your uncle is giving her the blues. She don't need you to give her a hard time, too. I'm not going to call her this time because I know that she's doing all she can. Besides, I don't want to worry that sweet, old lady. She's such a blessing to you, and you should thank God everyday for her. How's your mother doing?"

"She's somewhere, still sucking on a glass dick," I said,

becoming angry.

"I see. She's still on drugs, huh? Well, Demetrius, all you can do is pray for her, and she'll come around."

"Tell that to my granny because she's the one who is hurt by that bitch, not me."

I felt tears roll down my cheeks, and I didn't even know it. I was crying.

"It looks to me that it's hurting you, too. It's okay, son. You can cry. I cry sometimes, too. We all have feelings, and I understand what you're going through. My mother wasn't any different from your mother. I had to listen to her screw a different man every other night when I was a little boy."

"So, what are you saying? That your mama was a whore?"

"That's exactly what I'm saying. She had to do what she had to do, but social services removed me from her care and put me in foster care. She could have gotten a job and worked a nine-to-five. But she often told me, when I was a little boy, that she loved the fly by night money. I didn't know what she meant when I was younger, but, as I got older, I completely understood. She was a woman who sold her body for money, and she was on drugs, too. But, son, it's not where you come from, it's where you're going. And I see so much potential in you. You are one of my brightest students, and you remind me so much of myself. I grew up in foster care, and what kind of clothes do you think I wore? I didn't wear no name brand anything. But, for me, it wasn't about the clothes. It was about me making a difference. I wanted to grow up and get my mother off of drugs and take care of her. Unfortunately, that dream was shot to hell because her pimp shot her in the head. So, you see, son, there is not an easy street for no one. If there were an easy street, everyone's life would be peaches and cream."

I was sad for his mama and all, but I didn't want to hear

that sad-ass story that he had going on, so I tuned him out and thought about Ray Ray and Peanut's cars. Ray Ray had a box Chevy Caprice Classic with some twenty-six inch chrome rims on it. And Peanut had a bubble Chevy Caprice SS with twenty-four inch chrome rims. They had shiny gold jewelry, and they did everything together. They wore Versace silk shirts and Versace shades. Ray Ray was the oldest and the biggest. He was short and chubby with a Jeri curl. And Peanut was the opposite. He was tall and slim with a temp fade. They sold drugs together; they clubbed together. They even fucked girls together. They both had pull out gold teeth, and I wanted to be just like them. They made the hood look good.

Mr. James saw me in a daze and slammed a book on the desk to snap me out of my daydream.

"Listen to me, son. I have watched you ever since you were at that elementary school across the street. This is your last year, and I really want to see you graduate. You can be whatever you want to be. You have the potential to be the next president. Look at Barack Obama. He's a powerful black man, running this country. I bet he never dreamed of becoming the first black president. But he is, and look at him now. Son, there is no limit as to what God can do for you. All I need for you to do is believe. If you can believe it, you sure as hell can achieve it. I know you don't have the best clothes, and you're infatuated with those two nuts Ray Ray and Peanut. But, son, they probably won't even live to see thirty years old."

I looked at him and said it again, "Ray Ray and Peanut make the hood look good."

He grabbed my chin and said, "Son, everything that looks good isn't good. You have knowledge, and no one on God's green earth can take that from you. They might have flashy jewelry and cars, but they don't have a third of what you have, son. You have knowledge, and knowledge is power.

And your knowledge can lead you to become a doctor or a policeman. You could, maybe, even think about becoming a professional boxer. You have a mean right hook, and, maybe, you should take some of your frustration out in the boxing ring. I know Ray Ray and Peanut, and neither one of them would last five minutes in jail. And that's where they're headed if they don't stop selling those drugs. They only have two options, and those options are the jailhouse and the graveyard. So, ask yourself, do you really want to be like them, son? You can't see this now, but, trust me, you will understand everything that I am trying to tell you once you get older. What are you going to do once your granny's head turns cold? That lady is doing everything for you, and you act as if you don't care.

I was your age once, and I even got messed up with the wrong crowd. I ran away from the foster home and joined a gang. I had to steal a car to get initiated. They told me that, once I had stolen a car, I would be like their brother. I went to steal the car, but what they didn't tell me was that the owner of the car was at home. As I popped the lock with a slim jim, the alarm went off. I wanted to run, but I had no choice but to finish what I had started. Just as I was about to peel the steering column, the owner appeared at the driver's side window. He didn't hesitate to pull the trigger. I tried to run out of the passenger's door. But, as soon as I opened the door, I felt a hot blaze at my back. I ran so fast, and I knew that I had been shot, but my adrenaline was on full blast. That alone made me change my life. I went back to the foster home and obeyed the rules and worked and put myself through college.

"And I don't understand why I am alive today. I am supposed to be dead. I was in the hospital for about eight months. Now, ask me where my so-called gang brothers were? As far as they knew, I was dead because, when I got shot, they ran and left me. I could have died that night, but God had other plans for my life. I didn't want to be another statistic, but, at the rate I was going, I would have been dead by fifteen. This is what the so-called streets did to me," he said as he turned around to show me the gun shot blast to his back. Then, he said, "I used the same shitty-ass excuses that you are using now. But guess what, son? Everybody has problems, and no one wants to hear a sob story. I wanted a mother and a father, but I had to settle for a foster mother. Ms. Frost. And, boy, was she nice to me. I wanted stylish clothing and the best tennis shoes, but I had to settle for Kmart clothes. Son, if you don't remember anything that I have said to you today, always know that the difference starts with you. Self!," he said as he pointed at my chest. "Life isn't designed for us to get what we want. God has designed life for some of us to struggle, so we can be living testimonies for the next person."

I didn't know why he was telling me all of that black history shit because I had my mind made up. I was going to be a drug dealer like my idols Ray Ray and Peanut. I shook my head like I gave a fuck about his past.

"Do I really remind you of yourself?"

"As a matter of fact, you do. But I had a praying foster mother, and she never gave up on me. I know that you have a praying grandmother, and she loves you so much. Please don't bruise her heart anymore. It's already been broken by your Uncle Red and your mother. And if I can save one kid, I would really like for that kid to be you. I am not telling you about my hard times just for fun. Take heed to what I am saying, son. You really should consider becoming a boxer. I will even send you to boxing camp. This is your senior year, and I want you to further your education once you leave here."

"I hear what you're saying, but this is the nineties, and we're not in the sixties and the seventies. I got to get me some money," I said, irritated.

It was almost five o'clock. He had preached for damn near two hours.

"Son, the moral of the story is that the streets don't love you. The streets are good for nothing but swallowing you whole and spitting you out."

I looked at the clock again and said, "Is that it? Can I go now? I am ready to get back to the Bricks because Ray Ray and Peanut make the hood look real good."

"Boy, did you hear anything that I just said? You need to pay attention and listen to me and make it out of the hood."

I knew that Mr. James thought that he was just wasting his time with me, but, little did he know, that he had survived a gunshot wound just like my role model Ray Ray had done. I was somewhat infatuated with gun play.

Chapter 2: *Hard Times*

So, I just nodded my head and waited for him to finish telling me his story.

"Are you finished?"

"Go on ahead, Mr. Demetrius. Your grandmother is a good woman. You should want to make her proud, and what I mean by that is you should get your lessons and go to college. You can go to college because you and I have similar backgrounds. And look at me. You know that your grandmother is already having a hard time with your uncle. She's up in age, and anything is subject to happen to her."

I was so ready to get out of his class. I didn't want to hear that shit. I was going to make Granny proud alright. I was going to make some money to help her with our bills. He was talking about his childhood. Who cares about what went on in the seventies? We were living in a whole new era.

I waited outside for Kimmy. We always walked home together. I waited and waited, and finally I started walking by myself. I looked at my watch, and I noticed that it was almost six o'clock. *Time really flies when you're listening to bullshit, I* thought. *How does Mr. James know what my future is going to be like? Only God knows that, and, so far, it isn't looking too bright. It is shitty, and, so far, I am waiting for God to show up and show out. That's what my granny always says in her time of need.*

I liked walking back and forth to school because it gave me a chance to watch Peanut and Ray Ray on the block. They would be in their Chevy Caprices with the twenty-four inch rims and candy coated paint job. I wanted to definitely be a part of their entourage. As I walked by, they would honk their horns, and I would chunk up the deuces, thinking that I was going to be just like them someday. As I got closer to my house, I noticed that Granny was on the porch.

"What are you doing, Mama?"

I always called her Mama because she was the only mama that I knew, and Priscilla sure as hell didn't deserve to wear that title.

"Are you trying to catch you some fresh air, Mama?" I asked as I kissed her on her cheek. She had a worried look on her face, and I sensed that something was wrong, but I didn't know what. I sat on the steps and enjoyed watching the heavy traffic that headed to Peanut and Ray Ray's spot. Then, I heard her say with tears in her eyes, "Son, your loved ones will be the first to hurt you. You won't let a stranger hurt you because you won't let them get close enough. It always has to be blood." Then, she opened her Bible and said, "Son, I want you to love with your head as well as your heart."

She walked back in the house. I thought about what she had said as I stood there before walking in behind her. *I'm going to love with my head and become a mastermind at the dope game,* I thought. *I will get money by any means.*

When I walked in, I noticed that Granny was flicking a lighter, getting ready to light a candle. The sun was going down, and I really wasn't paying attention, until I walked in my room and turned on my light switch. Then, I noticed that our lights had been shut off.

"Granny, what happened to the lights? Your uncle came home drunk and let your mama in, and she stole the bill money off of my dresser. I asked Red why did he let her in, and all he said was that he don't even remember seeing her. I'd heard her voice when I was in the tub, but it was too late when I finally got out. She was in and out as quick as lightning. I don't see how those two turned out the way that they did. I kept those two in the church. Priscilla was doing good until she hooked up with your daddy. Now, she is so far gone off in them drugs that she hardly remembers anything. She don't even know if she's going or coming. And Red should be ashamed of himself. I spent my last putting him through college. I done got too old to worry about those two. I am sixty-eight years old, and I want to see sixty-nine. But, son, we're going to be alright. These candles and that gas stove will let us see some light until the first of next month."

I listened to her, and the more she talked about my mama and Uncle Red, the more I wanted to go rob a bank. My daddy wasn't any good either. I only saw him once a year, and that was at Christmas time. He got Priscilla hooked on drugs, and now he was clean and had started a new family and was living in the suburbs. *What a life*, I thought as I watched Granny prepare our dinner.

She fixed neck bones, lima beans, rice, and cornbread. We would always have a home cooked meal no matter what. I loved Granny's food. When we sat at the table, there was a knock at the door.

"I'll get it," I said as I got up.

I looked out the window and saw that it was Kimmy. She looked like she had been crying.

"What's wrong?" I asked as I unlocked the burglar door.

She sat on the sofa and began to cry. I just looked at her. I didn't know what to do. Her physical appearance looked to be okay, but her heart was hurting. She looked at me and said, "My dad died."

I didn't even know that she knew her dad because she had never talked about him, and now her daddy had just upped and died. He'd had a stroke.

My daddy and Uncle Red should have been the ones who died. Her daddy lived just south of Georgia, and he was supposed to come and get her for the summer.

"Come on in here and have some supper," Granny said. "The good ones are always the ones to go first," she said as she started to fix Kimmy a plate.

I thought, *Well, it looks like she'll be spending the summer with me.* She looked around and noticed all the candles that we had lit. I was embarrassed a little, but, then, I thought, *Shit happens.* She didn't say anything. She just poured hot sauce on her neck bones before she said her grace. *My kind of girl,* I thought. *If she eats dinner with me in the dark, I know that she'll be there for me when I get on my feet.* I watched her as she ate her food. I liked her so much, and I had the finest girl in school at my dinner table. After we ate dinner, we washed it down with some sweet iced tea.

I wished that there was something that we could do, like play my video game, but that was impossible, considering the damn lights were off. Instead, we sat on the porch and talked about our future. This was our last year in high school. She wanted to be a doctor, and I didn't know what I wanted to be, but I was going to be anything but BROKE! Now, I had to think of a way to help Granny get the lights back on. *We have to wait on her fixed income check in order for the lights to be back on. That's a long time,* I thought as I scratched the top of my head.

"What are you thinking about?" Kimmy asked.

"I'm thinking that I will have to get dressed in the dark for school tomorrow."

"You can stay at my house," she suggested. "My mother won't be home until ten in the morning."

"You know I can't leave Granny. She needs me here. Besides, I am all she's got. I got to get to this money. I am tired of being broke."

"Boy, you have to finish school first. You have to get an education first and use it and then get to the money that way."

She was starting to sound like our damn teacher. I tuned her out and focused my eyes on the souped up car that had just gone by. It was Peanut's bubble Chevy Impala SS, and his twenty-four inch chrome wheels were spinning as he drove by. There was always traffic in the Bricks. I enjoyed watching the crack heads get drugs from Peanut and Ray Ray. I, especially, liked the bank rolls that I had seen them fold up. The junkies had more money than I did, and I was sick of it. I was listening to Kimmy. She could use her education to make it, but I was going to use my mind.

It was getting late, so I decided to walk her home. I hollered in and told Granny to come and lock the burglar door. She stuck her head out the door and said, "Don't be out too late. This is a school night."

"I will be back, Granny. Just lock the door, so no one will come in on you."

"I hate it over here," Kimmy said as she grabbed my hand. "And those two stupid fools are going to be dead or in jail because no one has a future with drugs. You'll live for a little while, then it'll all start crumbling down."

She was talking about Peanut and Ray Ray. They looked like they were living pretty damn good to me. They had the Bricks on lock, and they had some of the finest bitches in the world.

"Do you want to come in?" she asked as she unlocked her door.

"Girl, your mama will kill both of us if she catches me in her house."

"That's just it. She won't catch us," she said as she pulled me in.

I'd never been in her house before. I had always stood on her front porch. When I walked in, I saw that there were pictures of Kimmy all over the walls. She had all types of certificates everywhere, from cheerleading to winning our school's spelling bee. *She sure could be a doctor,* I thought because she was very smart.

"Your granny sure can cook a good meal," she said as she turned on the living room light. I sat on the plastic covered love seat. "You can come back here with me," she said as she headed to her room.

Her room was neat. It wasn't messy like mine. She had a twin bed, and it was covered with a thick pink comforter. Her whole room was decorated in pink and white. As I looked around, I noticed that she had pink curtains on her window. I used a sheet for a curtain. *Pink must be her favorite color,* I thought as I sat on the edge of her bed. She walked over to her dresser and picked up a picture.

"This is my daddy," she said as she began to cry again.

I looked at the picture, and he looked like he was healthy. *But what does good health look like? There are people in their twenties having heart attacks,* I thought.

"I can't say that I feel your pain. But I am here for you. If you need anything, I will try my best to get it for you."

She hugged me, and the soft fragrance that she was wearing made me want her instantly.

"If you really want to be here for me, please stay with me until I fall asleep. You can lock the bottom lock. Please,

Black? I am in need of some company. I am grieving, and I am so down and out of it."

"I guess I could chill here for a little while."

"Great. I'll go take a shower and come right back. Please make yourself more comfortable," she said as she opened up her panty drawer.

I took off my hat and laid back on her bed. For some reason, I felt that she wanted to have sex. I could tell by her eyes. Plus, Granny had always told me, "These little hot tail girls will try to trap you. Girls are way more advanced than boys."

Little did Granny know that I had been fucking since I was thirteen. And how could Kimmy trap me? Because I didn't have shit. I didn't have a pot to piss in or a window to throw it out of. When she walked back in the room, she only had on a wife beater and a pair of boy shorts. I saw her pussy print.

She jumped on top of me and asked, "So, what are your plans when we get out of school?"

My brain couldn't think because my dick was standing straight up.

"Whoa," she said as she noticed my erection.

The silhouette of her body was perfect. There was steam still rising from her shoulders.

"I don't know," I said, looking down at my dick.

She knew what she was doing, and she was turning me on. She raised up my shirt and rubbed the hair on my stomach. I felt like I was getting ready to bust a nut. I sensed that she wanted to suck my dick because she began to caress my dick through my jeans. Then, she kissed my stomach.

"How long have we had a crush on each other now? About eight years?" she said as she unbuckled my jeans.

Whatever she wanted to do to me, I wasn't going to stop her.

"It's been about that long," I said as I rubbed my hand through her hair.

I never thought that this day would come. When she made her way up to my ears, she whispered, "I don't want to get pregnant."

"You're not going to get pregnant," I said as I grabbed her by the neck and kissed her endlessly. "I can pull out and skeet it on your ass. I don't have to cum in you."

"You mean to tell me that you don't have any condoms?" she asked.

"No. I don't have any condoms, and I don't need any. I'm not having sex with anyone.
Go check in your mama's room and see if she has any."

"Boy! My mama don't have sex!"

"How do you know? Everybody has to get their rocks off some kind of way."

"Well, maybe, you're right," she said as she left to go check her mama's room.

I took off my clothes and got under the covers. I grabbed my dick, and it was hard as ever. She came back with a condom.

"Does this mean that we're going to go together?" she said as she got under the covers.

"If you want us to," I said as I opened to condom.

"I never had sex before," she said as she eased out of her boy shorts and threw them on the floor.

"Don't worry. I won't hurt you."

I got on top of her and eased my dick into her tight pussy.

"Ouch!" she said as she slid back and reached for the headboard.

"That's just the head going in. Am I hurting you, baby? How does this feel?" I said as I eased the rest of my big dick inside of her.

She didn't say anything, but I felt her pussy grab hold of my dick. Then, it felt like my back was being ripped wide open. She scratched the hell out of my back as I pumped harder. Then, she looked at me smiled and said, "I always wanted to lose my virginity to you."

I kissed her, and we held each other as I continued to stroke. Her pussy was so tight, and it was feeling so good until I felt the condom tear. I wasn't ready to be a daddy, and I didn't want to fuck her future up with a child either. So, I said, "Do you have another condom?"

"No. Why do we need another one?" she said with a worried look on her face.

"Because I can feel that this one has torn. That's why it feels extra good," I said as my eyes rolled to the back of my head.

"Well, can you just pull out of me or something? Because it's feeling too good to stop."

"Yes, I could do that."

I was fucking her harder, and I was about to cum. Soon as I tried to get up, she wrapped her legs around me.

"What are you doing, Kimmy? I am about to cum, and neither one of us are ready for kids."

I had a feeling that she wanted me to cum in her and all I could do was think about what Granny had said about fast tail little girls. I wasn't ready to be a daddy. Hell! I was still wearing hand me downs to school. How in the hell could I afford a child? The more she threw her pussy back, the more sperm squirted in her pussy. My dick was still hard when she flipped me over and rode my dick like a cowgirl. She was riding my dick like she was no virgin.

"Just tell me when you're about to cum," she whispered.

"I already came."

"Well, let me know when you cum again," she said as

she rode my dick harder.

She was riding me and licking on her nipples at the same time. She blew my mind because no girl had ever done that in front of me before. I couldn't help it. I was about to cum again. *Can I have multiple orgasms with her? She sure can ride a dick,* I thought.

"I am about to cum again," I said through clenched teeth.

She jumped up just in time, but it was too late. The first nut had probably already reached an egg by now. I looked at her and said, "Are you sure that you were a virgin?"

Chapter 3: *Earning Stripes*

When it was all over and done, I was stunned at how good Kimmy rode my dick. She wasn't fooling me. She rode my dick like she'd had fucking lessons. I didn't know what to do next. I just laid there for a minute with cum all over my pubic hairs.

"You can take a shower if you'd like," she said as she got up.

I went to the bathroom and let the water run for a minute. I didn't know what it was about our water, but, in the Bricks, we had the hottest water ever. I stepped into the shower, and she joined me. *This girl has too much freak in her,* I thought as I adjusted the temperature of the water. Her body was so nice, and her skin complexion looked good up against mine. She was a thick red bone, which was just how I like my girls, and we looked good together. She got in front of me, and, as I looked at her sexy, round ass, my nature rose again. She turned around and began to bathe me softly and slowly. Every time she moved, her breasts moved, and my dick jumped. She made her way down to my dick, and, as the water ran on her face, she nibbled on my dick. I put my hands on the wall to balance myself as I watched her, sucking my dick.

"You like this?" she asked as she looked up at me.

"Hell, yeah!" I said as I moved her hair out of her eyes. "What are you trying to do to me?" I asked as I began to fuck her mouth.

"This has been a dream of mine, and I have always said, when I finally got you to myself, that this is what I would do to you."

She was jacking my dick and sucking it at the same time. I felt like I was about to fill her mouth up. Kimmy really took over in the shower. She really knew how to work her mouth, as well as her pussy.

"Let me bend you over," I said as I motioned for her to turn around. The moment was so intense, and neither one of us had a condom on our minds. She bent over, and I eased my dick in, and she didn't even cringe. She took all of my dick as I fucked her hard and fast from the back. Her ass was jiggling up and down as I slapped it. I was looking at my dick go all the way in and come all the way out.

She looked back and said, "Black, can you please cum in me again?"

How could I say no to her sexy ass in the hot, steamy shower?

"Please, baby. Your dick feels so good inside of me."

My dick was throbbing, and the more she begged for it, the closer I was to exploding all in her. Even my horny ass knew that it only took one time. One time to get pregnant and one time to catch AIDS! And I sure as hell didn't want any pussy taking me out of this world. I fucked her hard until I finally filled her pussy up. She turned around, kissed me, and said, "I want us to be together forever."

"That's cool," I said as I got a grasp of what had just

happened.

We got out of the shower and went back to her room. Time had flown by so fast, and I knew that Granny was probably worried sick about me. It was a little past midnight. *She sure had a funny way of mourning the death of her father*, I thought as I put on my Atlanta Falcons fitted cap. She wanted me to fuck her to death.

"I will see you in school tomorrow," I said as I headed for the door.

She hugged me and gave me a big kiss and said, "I hope I dream about you tonight." After saying our goodbyes, I waited as I heard her lock up. Just as I was about to bend the corner, I saw a boy holding a gun over someone who was lying face down on the ground. As I got closer, I noticed that it was Peanut, who was lying on the ground. He was getting robbed. It was pitch black, but there was a dim street light, and I stood there for a moment and heard the boy tell Peanut that he was going to put a bullet in the back of his head. I don't know what made me charge at the boy, but I rushed him, and the gun fell out of his hand. Peanut jumped up and grabbed the gun.

"I owe you one, homeboy," Peanut said as he dusted the red dirt off his Versace shirt. "Now, I got to deal with this fuck nigga who just robbed me," Peanut said as he hit the boy across the head with the gun.

I looked at the boy and saw that he was only a kid. He looked younger than me.

"I'm sorry, man. I was just practicing. I wanted to see how it felt to rob somebody."

"Nigga, do you see this five thousand dollar Versace shirt that you had me lying in the dirt in?"

He hit the boy in the head with the gun again. Then, he said, "As a matter of fact, you're going to take a little ride with me and my boy Black."

He still had the gun pointed at the boy's head.

"Black, let's roll. I am going to give you this gun, and, if this motherfucker looks at you wrong, you better squeeze it and put a few hot ones in his temple." Then, he turned to the boy and said, "And, little nigga, you get in the back seat."

"I got to go home. My granny is probably looking for me," I said.

"Look. Don't worry about her. I will pay your rent up for a whole year. I know your lights are off, too. I will go to Georgia Power personally first thing in the morning, so let's go," he said as he put the black Glock .40 in my hand.

What choice did I have? I had just saved one of my idols from getting a bullet put in the back of his head. *I've never held a gun before,* I thought as we both headed for the back seat. The boy had blood running down both sides of his face from the blows that Peanut had given him with the gun. Peanut turned his radio all the way up. He was playing Eightball and MJG's *Lay it Down. This can not be good,* I thought as I pointed the gun at the perpetrator. He was sweating and looked nervous as hell. *Why did he have to try and rob the hood's craziest nigga? And why did I have to get my stupid ass caught up in the mix? Granny is going to kill me,* I thought as I looked at Peanut, bobbing his head to the loud music that was playing.

If I was that dude, Peanut would have had to shoot me when he hit me in the head with the pistol. There was no way that I would have gotten in this car. It was just like being kidnapped, and we all know how kidnappings end up. Dead! Or, even worse, tortured. *Torture is the main thing that goes on in a kidnapping,* I thought. *Then, there's the possibility of getting buried alive.*

There was no telling what Peanut had on his mind. He was pissed off, and he was driving and rolling a blunt at the same time. He turned the radio down and said, "This little nigga just laid me down. Can you believe that shit, Black Boy?" He lit the blunt.

I had never held a gun before in my life, and I sure as hell had never shot anyone. The only thing I had shot were the men on my video game. I looked at the boy, and, even though he was just a kid, he was playing grown up games. He was sweating bad, and he had on a t-shirt that read THE DECK. He was from Decatur. I knew that he wasn't a Westside nigga because, if he was, then Peanut would have been dead. Westside niggas didn't do a lot of talking. Then, he opened up his mouth and said, "Hey, man. Please don't kill me. I was supposed to kill you to get initiated, so I could be in a gang. The Deck Boys Gang. They told me to rob you and bring them your money and gold chain."

"How the fuck does that sound?" Peanut asked as he pulled a strong puff from his blunt.

"It's true. I'm not lying. I swear."

"Little nigga, I'm going to tell you just like this. You should have killed me because we're about to kill your ass. You need a role model, huh? Well, too late for all that shit. You're about to make the statistics list — another dumb nigga not living to see age twenty-one. How old are you anyway, little nigga?"

"Sixteen," he said as he began to beg for his life. "Please don't kill me. I am sorry."

"You would have been better off linking up with me and my boys."

"But I'm from Decatur," he said as tears flowed heavily down his face.

"How do you feel about Decatur now... where it's not greater? I am going to kill you and bury your ass where nobody will be able to find you. So, how do you feel now, knowing that your stupid ass won't even have a funeral? You're going to be maggot food."

"Please don't kill me? Help!" he screamed.

"Little nigga, who the fuck can hear you over these sub woofers and amplifiers? Look around. We're in the middle of nowhere. Little nigga, did you forget that, less than thirty minutes ago, you had a gun to my head? I was minding my own business in my own hood, and here your punk ass came, robbing me. First, you said that you were practicing. Now, you say you want to be in a gang. Which lie is it? It don't matter because, either way, your life is going to end tonight. You can't practice in the real world. You only get one shot at life, and it looks to me like you fucked that up. God gave you life, and, now, I'm about to take your life from you. That gun that my partner Black is holding back there is real! This Versace shirt is real, and, now, it's covered in red dirt! See, I am from the Westside, born and raised. And, when a Westside nigga gets robbed, well...almost gets robbed...we have to handle business. We have to see to it that the fuck nigga pushes daises. And, in this case, you're that young fuck nigga. See, this isn't a movie, nor is this a script. You cannot pause and rewind what you just tried to do to me. Now, unfortunately, you have to suffer the consequences. You're about to pay with your life."

"I won't try to rob you again. Please don't kill me. I told you that I had to do it to be in the Deck Boys."

"How in the fuck did y'all pussy-ass Decatur niggas find me anyway?"

"They dropped me off and told me what kind of car you had. So, I waited until you came out. They told me that you were always flashy and that you would be wearing plenty of jewelry. Look at all that ice around your neck. You're not that hard to find."

"I know that, little nigga, but what I mean is, why the fuck they picked me?"

"The leader of the gang picked you and told me that I

had to do it. I just want to eat like you're eating."

He was starting to sound like me because that was all I wanted to do was eat, too, but I wasn't stupid enough to rob Peanut or Ray Ray.

"Little nigga, fuck a gang! That gang life don't pay your fucking bills. All they do is go around doing dumb shit like shooting and robbing innocent people. This pays your bills," he said as he held up a brick of cocaine. "Little nigga, what's your name?"

"Trevino," he answered nervously.

He looked at me. I was still pointing the gun at him.

"Don't look at me. I have the heart to squeeze this motherfucker," I said.

I saw Peanut look at me and smile through the rearview mirror. I was scared as hell, too, but I couldn't let Peanut know it. I was just talking tough in front of Peanut. I wasn't going to squeeze shit.

"You tried the wrong nigga, and, like he said, your stupid ass has got to learn." I shocked my damn self when I said that.

"That's what I'm talking about," Peanut said as he dumped ashes from his blunt into the ashtray. "I could use a nigga like you on my team, but your grandmamma is so damn strict."

"You have a grandmamma?" Trevino asked as he looked at the gun. "What's it like?"

I was at a loss for words. Here I was, holding a gun to a kid's head, who didn't have a clue about life. Period! But he was definitely on the wrong side of Interstate I-20 tonight.

"Never mind all of that, and your ass will never know," Peanut said as he passed me the blunt.

I had never smoked a blunt before, but I had to look cool in front of Peanut. I puffed it, and my throat immediately filled up with thick smoke. I had hit it too hard, and, as a result, I coughed really hard. I felt like I was choking. As I was coughing, Trevino dived at me, and, before I knew it, I pulled the trigger. Just like that, blood splattered all over the back seat and on me, as well.

Peanut looked back at me and said, "That was going to happen sooner or later because I was going to kill the little nigga myself."

He pulled into a twenty-four hour car wash. He didn't seem scared or nothing. This was like an ordinary thing for him.

He got out of the car and said, "Help me put this little nigga in the trunk."

Trevino was bleeding from his head very badly, and I felt like I had to throw up. After we threw him in the trunk, I felt like I needed some air. It was a winter night, but I needed air-conditioned air. He grabbed a bunch of brown paper towels to soak up the blood in the back seat. He sprayed Windex on the windows and wiped the excess blood that was dripping.

"Look at this shit!" Peanut said as he continued to wipe the windows. "I hate when this shit happens."

"You mean, this has happened before?"

"Not in my car, but I have definitely had to peel back a cap or two. But, Black, you got heart, though."

"Granny. She is going to kill me for sure because I have a murder on my hands," I said as I looked around to make sure no one else was at the car wash.

"She's not going to find out. We're going to bury this little nigga in the perfect spot," he said as we both got back in the car. "It's little niggas like that fool in my trunk that go missing every day. And you even said it yourself that he tried the wrong nigga."

After he finished speaking, Peanut rolled another blunt.

"What if the Deck Boys come looking for him?"

"Then, we'll have a war on our hands, and they asses can get it, too. My heart don't pump Kool–Aid, and there ain't shit soft and pussy pie about me. And, besides, by the time they find this fool, it will be years from now. He will be unrecognizable. I am taking him to that street where a white lady's body was found years after she went missing. A whole year had went by and the sorry-ass APD finally found her skeletal remains under cardboard and debris. One of her assailants even got the death penalty."

"The death penalty?" I repeated.

"But don't feel bad. It seems like everyone is going to get murdered in their lifetime anyway. No one has love for one another, and everyone is out for themselves. Every time I turn on the news, it's about how some dumb niggas has gotten shot by another dumb nigga. Either they're dying at the hands of another black male or at the hands of a dirty-ass police officer. No one is living to be grandparents anymore, so you should thank God everyday for your praying grandmamma. Everyone is living for the moment. No one is planning for the future. Now, don't worry. We're about to dump this little nigga because I got some hoes to pick up. The Westside is the best side," he said as he turned off the headlights and crept down a dark street.

He was so nonchalant about this whole ordeal. *I could get the death penalty,* I thought as my heart began to do numbers in my chest. He parked the car and turned off the lights. There were so many thoughts and voices running through my head, and Granny's voice was the main voice I heard. *I wish I would have taken Kimmy up on her offer and spent the night with her. I could be holding her right now and be in some pussy, but instead I am out on a homicide,* I thought.

We grabbed Trevino out of the trunk and threw him in a shallow ditch and covered him with some leaves.

"I thought that we were going to bury him in the ground or something," I said.

"No. This is cool," Peanut said as he kicked Trevino's arm into the shallow grave.

Then, he looked at me and said, "Don't start bitching up now. What's done is done. No one is going to find him because the sorry-ass APD don't look for wild-ass teenagers."

He had a point, but, as we drove off, I could have sworn that I saw the leaves move.

Chapter 4: *Not a Good Look*

The ride back home was silent. I wanted an ass whooping by Granny now because that was better than getting locked up for murder. I could hear her voice in my head now, saying, "Boy, trouble is easy to get into and hard to get out of." She always said, "Don't you go out there and get in no mess that you can't get out of."

Peanut was on his cell phone while I was in the passenger seat, sweating bullets. I had so much shit going through my head that I felt like I was about to die. I was that scared! I could have been in some pussy if I'd stayed at Kimmy's. I knew she was probably at home, up under her comfy covers, having sweet dreams. And my ass was riding with a gangster who hadn't said one word about the homicide that we'd just committed. It must have been after four in the morning, and he was carrying on a conversation with a girl on the phone.

"Look, bitch! I know that I am late, but I had to take care of some business," he said as he passed me the blunt.

This damn blunt is the reason why I shot Trevino in the first place, I thought as I puffed it and inhaled the smoke through my nose like I had seen Peanut do. This was my last year in high school and all I could think about was being shackled in an orange jumpsuit and hauled off to the Rice Street jail.

"You did the right thing," Peanut said as he adjusted the volume of the loud music that was playing. He took off of his chain and gave it to me.

"This diamond necklace is for me?" I asked. "Is this real?"

"Now, what kind of question is that?" he said as he parked in front of his trap house. "This costs about ten g's, and I want you to have it. You actually saved my life."

"I just acted off of natural instinct, I guess," I said as I looked at the medallion and platinum chain. The medallion was a crown that was embezzled with diamonds.

"One last thing," he said as he turned off the ignition. "You can't say anything to anyone about what happened tonight."

"I'm not going to tell anyone," I said as I looked around.

"On the West Side, we live by the G-CODE. You are a gangster now. You did some player shit. I mean I was going to shoot the little nigga in the head anyway, so don't feel bad, okay, Black? You did what you felt was necessary. A nigga charged at you, and you had to put the steel on his ass. Now, come on up here and let me give you a little something extra for your troubles because I know Granny is about to go upside that head when you get in the house."

"Umm, that's okay. I really must be going."

He went in his pocket and handed me all of the cash that he had in there. I was shocked! I'd never had over five dollars before. I got out of his car and started to walk to my apartment. Then, it dawned on me that I had blood all over me. I quickly turned around and said, "I can't go in the house covered in blood. Look at my shirt."

"Come on. Let's go upstairs and get you cleaned up."

When we got upstairs, I saw that the trap house had black everything, from the blinds to the furniture to the rug. The walls were even painted black. I looked around and noticed that Ray Ray wasn't there. *Where could he be?* I wondered as I headed to the bathroom. I didn't know if I was starting to feel the effects of the weed or what because I wasn't moving very quickly. I was moving in slow motion. Now, all I could hear was Mr. James telling me, "Marijuana kills the brain cells." I looked at myself in the mirror, and I thought about what Peanut said. He had said that I was a G.

After I took a quick shower, Peanut said, "You don't have to worry about these clothes. I'm gonna burn them. Here. Throw these on."

When I left, I was looking like a drug dealer. Peanut, also, gave me his cell phone number and told me that he owed me one. I looked at the sky as I headed home and saw that the day was about to break. I took off the heavy chain and put it in my pocket. *This has, indeed, been the longest day of my life,* I thought.

When I reached to open the door, Granny opened it for me.

"Where on God's green earth have you been, boy? I was worried sick about you! Are you hurt?" she said as she walked towards me, holding a candle in my face.

"No, Granny. I'm not hurt. I fell asleep at Kimmy's."

"Well, you only have about an hour to get ready for school. I am about to fix you some breakfast."

I was so glad that the lights were off, so Granny couldn't see the new gear that I had on. I laid across my bed and closed my eyes. They were so heavy. All I needed was an hour's worth of sleep. I didn't have an appetite; I needed some sleep. I was nervous and still high all at the same time. I grabbed some clothes out of the drawer and put them on. I walked out the door and headed to school.

When I got to school, I was the center of attention as usual. But, today, the kids weren't laughing with me, they were laughing at me. They were laughing at my wrinkled clothes. They looked like I had gotten them out of the dirty clothes hamper. As I walked to my seat, I looked over to where Kimmy normally sat, but she wasn't there. I had so much on my mind. I didn't have time for the bullshit today.

Lenny was the cool kid, and he sat in the back. He wore the latest fashions like Tommy Hilfiger and Jordan tennis shoes. When he started clowning my clothes, saying that they looked dirty, I looked back and gave him a devious look dead in his eyes. He ignored my ass whooping look and continued to amuse the class by talking about my shoes and clothes. Everyone laughed at the things he said. But no one knew my situation. Their lives were peaches and cream, and mine was pork and beans without the weenies.

After I took all I could take of Lenny's mouth, I stood up and threw my chair at him. He charged at me, and I took all of my frustration out on him—the lights being off, my mama stealing the bill money, my regrets about my night with Peanut, and everything else that was bugging me. He was funny, but he couldn't fight worth shit.

Mr. James made his way through the crowd and broke us up. I was relieved that Kimmy wasn't there to hear Lenny shining on me. When Mr. James pulled us apart, Lenny was breathing hard and looking mad. I didn't feel bad that he had a busted lip and a knot on his head. I was the wrong nigga to fuck with. Mr. James looked at me and told me to go to Ms. Williams' office.

"I can't keep tolerating you interrupting my class. I am tired of wasting my time trying to talk some sense into your head."

"That's just it," I said. "You don't know what's going on inside of my head." As I walked out, I yelled, "Fuck this class!"

As I walked to the principal's office, I thought, *Granny is going to kick my ass.* Ms. Williams had told me that, the next time she saw me in her office, I was going to have to go to an alternative school. She was going to kick me out of Bankhead High.

I walked as slow as I could, trying to think of a lie that I could tell her. But I was going too slow because Mr. James' black power ass came flying right behind me. I thought, *I should have just skipped school today.*

"How hard is it for you to follow the school's rules, huh?" he asked.

"Man, school ain't making me no money, so why should I listen to what y'all have to say?"

"Things you go through today will determine your tomorrow. Don't you get it, son?"

"Whatever," I said as I opened the door to the office.

"Good morning," Mr. James said to the secretary as we entered the office.

She looked me up and down and cracked a smirk to herself.

"This is just another day in class with Black, I mean, Demetrius," he said sarcastically. "Is Ms. Williams in?"

"She sure is. You all can go on back."

He instructed me to walk in first.

"Mr. James and Mr. Demetrius, what can I do for you two?"

"Well, it seems as though Demetrius can't keep his hands to himself."

"Is that right?" she said as she walked to her file cabinet

to retrieve a manila folder with my name on it.

The folder was thick. It was thick like Granny's food stamp folder at the welfare office.

"I've given you chance after chance, and now you leave me no choice. You will be expelled for the rest of the year."

"But I am at the door of graduating. Plus, Lenny's pussy ass started the fight."

"Young man, I will not allow you to use such vulgar language in my office."

"Man, whatever," I said as I stormed out of her office.

This was the longest walk home because I couldn't think of a lie to tell Granny. Besides, I knew that the school officials were going to tell her that I had gotten expelled. As I walked, I heard loud music coming from behind me. When I turned around, I saw that it was Peanut.

"Jump in, Black. Let's go pay that bill and make your granny proud."

I thought, *If I pay the light bill, maybe Granny will go easy on my butt.*

Chapter 5: *Hanging with the Big Dog*

"I want you to know that you did some G-shit last night," Peanut said as I sat in the front seat.

I barely heard him because I was thinking about the pain that I would be causing Granny once she found out that I'd gotten expelled from school.

"I just acted out of natural instinct. I mean, you would have done the same thing for me," I said as I put on my seatbelt.

"G's don't wear seatbelts. Only squares wear them, so unhook that shit," Peanut said as he passed me the blunt. "No doubt I would have done the same thing for you."

I hit the blunt soft, blew out the smoke, and said, "My granny is going to kill me for sure now."

"She's not going to find out about last night."

"I'm not talking about last night. I got into a fight today, and I got expelled from school. I got expelled for the rest of the year, and graduation is only five months away."

Peanut quickly whipped a U-turn and said, "I gotcha, Black Boy."

"What are you going to do?" I asked, holding on as he

made that illegal U-turn.

"I'm going to pay Ms. Williams a little visit. There comes a time in life when you have to throw your weight around. I will not let you get to the door of graduation and just stop going to school. She owes me a little favor, and I'm sure she will think twice about expelling you once she sees my face."

We pulled back up at Bankhead High, blasting music, and all eyes were on us. I felt cool as hell, but I still looked like shit, considering what I had on.

"Sit tight, Black Boy. I will be right back," Peanut said as he headed to the main entrance of the school.

While sitting in Peanut's stylish car, I watched everybody as they watched me. At that very moment, I felt like I was in control. I felt very powerful. All the girls were looking at me, licking their lips, and I wasn't even driving. I was on the passenger side.

I watched Peanut as he came back to the car. His diamond necklace was swinging from side to side. He had a blunt in his ear. He was cool as hell. I wanted to be just like him.

"You're no longer expelled, Black Boy," he said as he got back in the car.

"You mean that mean-ass Ms. Williams is going to let me back in school? How did you do that?" I asked as I reached for the blunt that he had just lit.

"She's a functioning junkie, and I could strip her from her school's code of excellence."

"Are you trying to say that Ms. Williams smokes dope?"

"Hell, yeah!"

"But she's so sophisticated and smart and shit. She even drives a Benz to school," I said shocked as ever. "She's the school's principal."

I couldn't believe that she was a crack head.

"Those are usually the ones who get high. They are all high and mighty in your face, but then their demons start to show at night. She's been smoking crack ever since I went to Bankhead Elementary. My uncle used to sell her drugs. I used to open the door for her when she would come by our trap house late at night. She's still fine as fuck, though, and I would fuck her old ass any day. I remember seeing her come in with a long black trench coat with nothing on underneath. My uncle used to tell me that one day he was going to pass the dope game torch to me. And look at me now. He taught me well. I remember when my uncle used to come home on those late nights. He would be clubbing at Club 559, Club 731, and the Silver Fox. But the Silver Fox has been changed to Da Fox Phase 2. It's owned by two well known brothers, Danny Boy and Poo Poo. It is a club that we have to definitely check out on Friday nights. And they serve some hot, delicious food, too. But, yeah, my uncle was a G-ass nigga, too, and he didn't take no shit from nobody. I got the Bricks on lock, and I wish that he was here to see me now."

"Where is your uncle now?"

"He's in that big-ass sky, looking down on me. He got busted for twenty bricks of cocaine, and he was on his third strike. He was already on parole, and he was facing life in prison. He said that he was never going back to jail, so, on the night that he got busted by the undercover officers, he reached under his seat for his gun. He had a shoot out with the policemen, but it was a no win situation. When it was all over, they had riddled his body with over one hundred bullets. I was about fifteen years old, and I represented at his funeral. I bought the whole hood t-shirts with his picture on the front. By that time, I knew the trade of the dope game. He always taught me to never piss in my own pool. I never do dirt on my side of town. I take several trips to the country every now and then and fuck them country boys over. They don't know dope anyway. Black boy, life is just a game. And the name of the game is called *survival*. And all you have to do is survive as long as you're breathing. You have to do what you have to do in order to eat, in order for your family to eat. You feel me?"

"Yeah, I feel you," I said as I gave him a high five.

"Now, let's go in here and turn them lights back on."

He hit the alarm on his car, and we proceeded to walk into Georgia Power by the West End Mall. He didn't even wait in line. He just went to the counter and gave the receptionist one thousand dollars.

"Black Boy, come and give her your address," Peanut said as he put the rest of his money back in his pocket.

The lady looked at me and said, "Well, what is it?"

I looked around at all of the angry customers, who had been standing in the long line, then, I said, "2545 Bankhead Highway, Atlanta, Georgia 30318."

She handed me a receipt, and we left. Just as we were walking out of the door, an old black man looked at Peanut and said, "I hate your kind."

Peanut turned his hat to the back and said, "I hate your kind, too, old-ass bastard. I hate that y'all old-ass people drive slow as fuck. I hate that y'all old-ass people always preaching that black history shit. If that nigga Martin Luther King Jr. lived in the Bricks, he would have done what he had to do to feed his family, too. Coretta would have understood that he had to do what he had to do to get by. So, old-ass man, miss me with that bullshit. You old-ass motherfucker."

"I'm an old man. There's no doubt about that, but kids such as yourself aren't even making it to become old men."

"Man, if you weren't so old, I would punch you in your wrinkled-ass face," Peanut said as he walked out the door.

I slowly walked out behind him, and the old man said,

"You don't want to get messed up with a fellow like him. I see something in you," the old man said as I walked out of Georgia Power.

"Can you believe that old-ass bastard?" Peanut said as he changed the CD. "He don't know shit about me. How the fuck can he judge me?"

"Fuck that old-ass motherfucker," I said as I remembered not to put on my seatbelt. Granny had always taught me to respect my elders, and that old man did speak the truth, but I had to remain cool in front of Peanut. *Our black asses are dropping like flies every day,* I thought. *Look at Trevino. He just lost his life last night. And there's no telling how many more of us have died since last night.*

I stretched out in the seat and listened to T.I.'s song "Hurt".

"This nigga right here is real," he said as he turned up the volume. "I fuck with this nigga T.I."

We pulled into the parking lot of the Mall West End.

"I know that you get picked on at school and shit for those dirty-ass clothes that you have to wear." Peanut put the car in park and said, "Can you believe that old-ass motherfucker? Damn! I still can't get over that shit."

He turned off the ignition.

That old ass man must've struck a nerve because Peanut is still pissed off, I thought as I got out of the car.

"Come on. Let's go in here and get you about ten pairs of fresh, new kicks," Peanut said as he hit the alarm on his car.

"You mean, ten pairs of shoes?"

"Yes. Ten pairs of shoes," he said, looking down at the rundown Pony tennis shoes that I had on.

We went straight to Foot Locker. I had always wanted a pair of Michael Jordan tennis shoes.

"Pick out what you want, Black Boy," Peanut said as

he went to flirt with the cashier.

When it was all over, I had Retro, Flight, Melo, Alpha, Fly Wade, Jumpman, and Air Max Jordans. I even got a pair of Jordan Hydro slippers and two pairs of Timberlands.

He said, "You don't have to be from up north to rock a pair of Timbs."

I, also, grabbed two pairs of Polo boots. He cashed out with a grand total of $2000. He even gave the cashier a two hundred dollar tip.

"I can't keep all of these shoes at home," I said as we headed to the car.

"You can keep them at my trap spot. I know how your granny is, and the lights should be back on by now."

We put the bags in the trunk and got back in his car.

"Now, we got to go to Lenox Mall to get you some clothes to wear with all those shoes," Peanut said as he hopped on Interstate 20.

I reached for my seatbelt and he said, "If you'll feel more comfortable, then wear the motherfucker."

I wanted to wear my seatbelt because, in my driver's education class, I watched films on how you could end up if you didn't wear your seatbelt. I even saw that some people who had been ejected from cars because they weren't wearing their seatbelts. If they would have worn their seatbelts, they would probably be alive today.

"Black Boy, I look at life like this— when it's my time to go, I'm going to go, and no seatbelt is going to save me."

He did have a point because my granny always said, "When God is ready for you, He's coming." She'd, also, say, "You can run all you want, but you can't hide from God."

When we pulled up at Lenox, he threw the keys to the valet attendant and said, "Don't wreck my shit."

"Yes, sir," the valet said as he caught the keys.

My eyes were so big. I had never been to Lenox Mall before. Hell, I'd never even been to Greenbriar Mall before. There were so many people in there. It seemed like everyone had shopping bags, even the kids.

"Where do you want to go first?" Peanut asked.

"I don't know anything about a mall," I said as I looked around at the high escalators. "I want to rock some of that fly shit that you wear."

"I wear a lot of fly shit. I rock True Religion, Versace, and Red Monkey Jeans."

"Do you like Polo, too?" I asked as we walked into Macy's.

"They have plenty of Polo in here," Peanut said as he looked over to see if there were any women at the cash register.

"I fuck white hoes, too," he said as he headed to the cashier.

"Can I help you?" an extra friendly gay man asked me. "You are a tall, glass of dark chocolate milk," he said as he looked me up and down. "I can get past those raggedy-ass clothes,"

I looked behind me because I knew that this punk-ass nigga wasn't hitting on me.

"Who the fuck are you calling a tall glass of dark chocolate milk? Nigga, I will break your face," I said as I ran towards him.

He turned and ran so fast that he knocked over several mannequins as he tried to get away from me. I grabbed a few Polo shirts, sweaters, and jeans. When I met up with Peanut, he was at the register, flirting with a snow bunny.

"You straight, Black Boy?" he asked as he pulled out a wad of money.

"I'm straight as an arrow," I said as I mean mugged the gay sales associate from earlier.

"I'm going to call you, Britney," he said as he paid for my clothes. "You can never have too many bitches," Peanut said as he helped me with my bags. "I got a bitch for everything. I got a bitch who lets me fuck her in the ass. I got a bitch that sucks on my dick all night long. I tell my bitch who don't let me fuck her in the ass that my other bitch will. And now I will add that snow bunny to my team. And those white bitches swallow all the nut out of a nigga's dick."

His talk was so cool, calm, and collected. He was such a cool-ass nigga, and I idolized the fuck out of him.

We went to valet and got in his car. He gave the valet attendant a twenty dollar bill. We threw the bags in the back seat.

"The next stop will be Phipps right across the street. That's where we can get the Trues and the Versace."

He turned up the music once again, and we were both bobbing our heads to the raw music of the rapper T.I. When we pulled up at Phipps, he did the same thing. He threw the keys to the valet and said, "Don't wreck my shit."

When we walked in Phipps, we passed by the Gucci store. I had never seen Gucci on anything but the internet. We went on the other side and went into Saks Fifth Avenue. I already knew what to do, so I looked around to see what I wanted, while he shot to the front to see who was at the cash register. As I looked at the True Religion jeans, I noticed that they all looked tight. I didn't want to wear anymore nut huggers if I didn't have to. I strolled to the back of the rack and found some that read Bobby Straight leg.

"Whoever the hell he is," I said to myself as I grabbed five pairs in my size. "And who the fuck is Samuel?" I said as I grabbed a couple of True Religion Cargo shorts. "I don't know neither one of these niggas, but I'm going to wear this shit." I grabbed a few t-shirts and headed to check-out.

When I got up there, Peanut was flirting with an older woman.

"Hold up. Did you get a nice jacket?" he asked as he thumbed through the clothes on my arms.

He went to the back and brought back a Versace Andrew Marc cognac colored leather jacket. I didn't see anything Versace that I wanted because it looked like Peanut had all of the Versace shirts that I saw.

"There. That will set those Timberland and Polo boots off," he said as he laid the jacket on the counter. "This is a Tumbled Westside jacket and, you're a Westside nigga, so I had to grab it for you."

My black ass didn't know style or fashion if it bit me in the ass. He pulled out his money and paid for my things. He looked at the older woman and said, "I'm going to call you, Miss Lady."

She was grinning from ear to ear. His gold teeth were shining as he talked to her, and she was just smiling, too. As we walked out, he looked at me and said, "Old hoes need love, too. My dick don't discriminate."

I really liked Peanut, and I respected and appreciated all that he was doing for me. He gave the valet attendant a twenty dollar bill, and we got in the car and headed back to the Bricks.

"I really appreciate all of the nice things that you bought me."

"It's not a problem. After all, I owe you my life," he said as he turned the music down lower.

Chapter 6: *Back in the Bricks*

Peanut had rolled so many blunts from Buckhead to Bankhead that I eventually lost count. I was high as hell. I was so happy that I was no longer going to go to school looking like a bum off the streets. I couldn't wait to see the look on Lenny's face when I got back to school after winter break. *I am going to be fresher than a fool*, I thought.

When we pulled back in the Bricks, Peanut parked at the back door to his trap house. He hollered up for a couple of his junkies to help us with my bags.

"Y'all better not even look in these bags," he told them as they headed down the steps. "Speedy, I want you watch these other motherfuckers," he said as he looked around at the junkies, grabbing my bags.

"I gotcha, boss," Speedy said as he grabbed a few of my bags.

"Come on, Black. Follow me."

When we walked in his apartment, there were several girls sitting on the sofa.

"Be excused," he said as he motioned at them to get off

the sofa and go to the back. "Have a seat, Black," he said as he walked to the refrigerator. "Do you want a cold one?"

He held up a double deuce Budweiser.

"No, I am good."

"Suit yourself," he said as he opened up his beer. He sat down and turned on the TV. "What do you want to watch?" Peanut asked as he flipped through the channels. He tossed me the remote, and I started turning to different channels. Granny couldn't afford cable, so all we watched at home was the news and *Wheel of Fortune*. My granny loved herself some *Wheel of Fortune*.

I was flipping through channels and came across a music video channel.

"Leave it right there," Peanut said as he grabbed the other remote to turn the volume up. "That's my nigga T.I. They can say what they want to say about him, but I fuck with his music. I don't care if he's from Cobb County or Bankhead, he's a real nigga, either way it goes."

I sat there and just glanced around at everything that he had in there. There were Pyrex pots everywhere, along with a box full of baking soda. There seemed to be a gun everywhere my eyes looked. There was a gun on the entertainment center. There was a gun on the coffee table. There was a big gun hanging on the wall behind the front door.

Even though we lived in the same apartments, his seemed to be a little bigger.

"Where do you want us to put these bags, boss?" Speedy asked as he and the other junkies headed in.

"Put them in the very back, in the third bedroom."

That explains why his apartment looks bigger than mine. He has a three bedroom, I thought. I watched them as they carried my bags.

"These are yours," he said as he threw me a set of house

keys. "You can come here and change clothes whenever you need to. I know you can't put on all of that fly shit at home."

"You're right about that," I said as I watched the junkies head to the door.

"They're all back there, boss. I even hung the clothes up and lined the shoes up," Speedy said.

"That's cool," Peanut said as he threw him a bag of crack.

"What about us?" one of the other junkies asked. "What do we get?"

"You get to live. Now, get the fuck out!" Peanut looked at me and said, "When you get down with my team, you will have to put junkies in their place. They will always try and get over on you. But I have Speedy in charge of my building."

"You have this whole building? But I thought that you and Ray Ray shared an apartment."

"Ray Ray has the building behind mine. We used to share this one, but, as we expanded, there was no need to share."

Peanut walked to the back and told the girls that he would see them later. He told them that he would call them tomorrow.

"So, what do you want to do, Black? It's the weekend, and you got all of that fly shit back there." He locked the burglar door behind the girls as they left. "Do you want to go to the club with me tonight? We could go to Club Crucial. That's T.I's club. Or we could just go to Buckhead and fuck around. I love going to Buckhead and showing off in front of those white folks."

"I wish I could go. That sounds like fun, especially T.I's club. But my granny would kill me," I said as I watched a video on the TV.

"I'll have a talk with your granny," he said as he went to go answer the door.

He told the man at the door to go downstairs and holler

at Speedy.

"I know my granny, and she's not going to let me out of her sight."

"Let me handle it. Money talks and bullshit walks."

"You can't pay my granny off. She'll never go for that. I'm not going to pay your granny off. I'm just going to make her an offer that she can't refuse."

I didn't know what he meant, but I didn't like the sound of it. My granny and I used to sit on our porch and watch Peanut and Ray Ray serve drugs. She'd always say, "Those two are going to end up dead or in jail." *She always told me not to get involved with them, and look at my black ass. I am already tied to a murder with one of them,* I thought.

"She's probably worried sick about me right now," I said as I continued to watch TV.

Then, he looked at me and said, "Well, at least, she's worrying about you with the lights on. How old are you anyway?"

"I'm seventeen. I will be eighteen in March, on the fourteenth."

"No shit! Are you for real? That's my birthday, too." He showed me his driver's license. "No wonder we clicked like a seatbelt," Peanut said as he jumped up to give me high five. "So, let's get something straight right now. We know each other like the back of our hands, especially since our birthdays are on the same day. I only have one rule, and that's to remain loyal at all times. Don't ever lie to me. If you feel that you need to lie to me, then I would rather you didn't say shit at all."

"I will never lie to you."

"That's what I wanted to hear," he said as he turned the TV off. "Now, let's go and have a talk with your granny."

Chapter 7: *My Granny Wasn't Born Yesterday*

After we left Peanut's trap house, he told me to wait in the car. I sat in the car and watched him go downstairs to the other apartment. He gave Speedy a kilo of cocaine. *He must really trust him,* I thought as I watched the other junkies come forward like roaches did to a piece of cornbread. It really amazed me how drugs could take over people's minds. And one of those people was my mama. I couldn't shake it out of my mind. *How many times have I seen her high?* I wondered.

Her eyes were always big and wide open. She used to sneak in our apartment, while we were all asleep, and peep over us to see if we were actually sleep. One day, I pretended to be asleep, and I watched her as she fondled my granny's bosoms, looking for money. She took all of Granny's money. Granny had to take medication for having high blood pressure, and she could sleep through a tornado. I didn't say anything. I got back in my bed and laid there and waited for her to come and kiss me. That was something good that I could remember about her. She wasn't much of a mama, but she made sure she kissed me when she was having her crack binges. I would lay there squeezing my eyes tight, like I was sound asleep, and then her strong alcoholic breath would hit me dead in my face. She would say, "I do love you, son. Mama is just going through some things right now." I never told her that I loved her back because I knew that she didn't mean it.

Granny showed me love, and I knew she meant it. She would tell me all through the day that she loved me. She would tell me when she woke me up for school. She would tell me on my way to the bathroom to brush my teeth. She would tell me at breakfast. She would tell me every morning when I left for school. She would tell me when I walked in the door from school. She would even tell me that she loved me while she was beating my ass. She would say, "Son, if I didn't love you, I wouldn't beat you." I didn't see the logic of it, but she was my granny, and I believed everything that she said. And she has not stirred me wrong, thus far.

Every time I sat back and reminisced about my mama, I always got very mad. I felt that she should have been a better woman and talked to me, her only son. But I was doing damn good to have lived in the Bricks and not even been to juvenile. That was because my granny didn't let me out of her sight. Our daily routine was school, church, and watching *Wheel of Fortune*. On Sundays, Granny and I would walk to the corner church. I really didn't like going to church because I had to wear fly collars and bell bottoms. But now it had become a fashion statement, and I saw that people were bringing everything back.

Granny don't have her strength like she used to, but, when she did, she didn't let me get away with shit. Whenever I got in trouble at school, she didn't wait until after she cooked dinner. She went across my head right then and there. There were times when I would be mad at her after she went to work on my behind. But after a few minutes or so, I would come out of my room and join her as she watched *Wheel of Fortune*. She used to tell me that she wanted me to grow up and be a respectable, productive, young black man. For the most part, I think that I am doing a damn good job of staying out of trouble.

I had been reminiscing so long that I didn't even notice that Peanut had gotten in the car. He didn't go straight to my apartment. He rode around first, and we rode past Kimmy's building. I saw that she was sitting on the porch. She looked over at me with a surprised look on her face. She never knew me to hang out with him. I wanted to stop and ask her why wasn't she in school today, but I knew that I would catch up with her later. Peanut turned the music down as we approached my building. Granny was sitting on the porch, waiting for me. When I got out of the car, she just looked at me and didn't say anything.

"Hey, Granny," I said as I sat on the second step on our porch.

"Don't 'hey' me," she said as she looked at Peanut, still sitting in his car. "What are you doing with that criminal?"

"It's not like that, Granny. I did a favor for him, and he returned the favor and paid our light bill."

"You mean to tell me that a drug dealer paid my bill? What favor did you do for him?"

"I washed all of his cars, and he said that he really liked the way that I shined his rims."

She looked at Peanut as he walked up and said, "Do you two fools think that I was born yesterday? I appreciate you paying my light bill. I will pay you back on the first of the month."

"It's not a problem at all," Peanut said.

"I'm not finished," she said as she fanned herself faster. "I do not want to see my grandson around you ever again! Do you hear me? Now, get away from here before a bullet that is meant for you comes and strikes one of us. Demetrius, go on in there and draw you a bath."

"But,Granny!"

"But nothing! Demetrius, go now!" She looked back at Peanut and said, "Get away from my apartment right now."

As he walked to his car, he said, "You know, one day, you're going to have to let him fly on his own."

"He will fly when I die," Granny said as she came in the house.

Chapter 8: *The Older, the Wiser*

I went to my room, and Granny followed me shortly after.

"Son, I don't know how many times I have to tell you that those guys are up to no good."

Granny grabbed my hand. She was a tiny, little lady with such a big heart. She stood at about five feet tall. She was a little old something, but she didn't play about me getting in any trouble either. Even though I was almost six feet tall, that didn't matter. When it was time for her to go across my head, she did. She didn't care what she threw either. I remember, one time, she called me in her room to turn off the light.

I said, "You called me in here for that?"

But I should have been more considerate since she had just gotten out of the hospital. As soon as I walked away after turning off the light, she threw her Crawford Long Hospital mug and hit me dead in the back of my head. I didn't talk back. I just took the lick and went and finished playing my video game. I was all into it, so that was why I didn't want to be bothered. *But I love my granny, though,* I thought.

As I laid back on my bed, I noticed that it was wet.

"What the fuck?" I said as I jumped up.

Then, the strong odor of piss hit my nose. It was bad enough that we had to share a room, but we had to share a damn twin bed, too.

"Sorry for my grammar," I said to Granny as I went to go find Uncle Red.

It couldn't have been nobody but him. He was always coming in there, smelling and talking like a walking alcoholic. I went to look for him around the house. Then, I found him in the front room, lying on the sofa, face down, asleep. He was pissy-ass drunk. I wanted to knock him across his head, but Granny had always said that I could kill him since he was heavily under the influence of alcohol. We had fought plenty of times, and we fought mainly because he was a damn drunk.

"I meant to tell you that he was back," Granny said as she walked in after me.

"Get your pissy self up," I said, trying not to curse again in front of Granny.

"Leave him alone," Granny said. "Let him sleep it off."

"Look at his clothes. He's getting piss on the couch."

"It's an old couch anyway. Now, just take a shower and sleep in my bed tonight."

"I can't sleep in your bed. I will just blow up the air mattress that Priscilla uses when she's here."

"We will finish our conversation," I heard Granny say as I walked back into my room.

I pulled the pissy sheets off of my bed and put them in a plastic bag. It would have been a lot better if we had a washer and dryer, but we didn't, so I had to do what I had to do. I looked out of my window and saw that a fight was going on. I couldn't tell who was fighting, and I didn't care to find out. I was already knee deep in some bullshit anyway. Then, I heard shots ring out. I hit the floor like I had been doing all my life. Granny had always taught me, when I was much younger, to always hit the deck when I heard something go pow pow.

"You alright in there?" I heard Granny say.

"Yes, I am good. Are you alright?" I shouted back.

I peeped up and looked out the window, and everyone was gone.

"You can get up now, Granny," I said as I brushed my pants off. "It was just some fools fighting and shooting. They probably didn't even shoot nobody."

"That's what I mean when I tell you to watch the crowd that you're with because this generation coming up now is all a bunch of damn fools."

She walked in and headed to the bottom of my bed and proceeded to flip the mattress over.

"I got it," I said as I strong armed the mattress and flipped it over.

"I don't know what this world is coming to," Granny said as she looked out of my window. "But I do know one thing. I will not allow you to hang around these no good hoodlums. I will not lose you to these mean-ass streets," Granny said as she walked out of my room.

I didn't want to hear that "losing me to the streets" shit anymore. I had survived this long.

I was so pissed off about Uncle Red and his piss stains all over the dam house. Uncle Red had been a bum ever since I realized that he was my uncle. He was family, but what does family mean when every family member is separated and doing their own thing? Either someone was on crack or someone was a damn alcoholic. Granny had such a big heart, and she would feed or house damn near everyone that she came into contact with. Priscilla wasn't good for nothing but coming in after her crack binges, stealing Granny's bill money. And look at Uncle

Red's smelly ass.

I didn't see why she didn't just block him from coming back in the house, but she had always said that Uncle Red would be her son until the day that he died. She had, also, told me on numerous occasions to never turn my back on family. Granny was always preaching that religious shit. I wondered, *Why did Priscilla turn her back on me?*

Chapter 9: *Living for the Weekend*

The winter break was approaching, which meant that I would be out of school for a couple of weeks. I really wanted to hang with Peanut and go to the club. He made it sound like so much fun. I didn't care where I went because all I knew was going to church and the candy lady. And I couldn't go to the candy lady unless there was one near our building. Granny didn't allow me out of her eye sight— period. I kind of had a little leeway now since I walked to and from school. I hadn't given Granny a reason not to trust me. I was bored and tired of playing my video game. I walked to the front room and saw that Granny was watching *Wheel of Fortune*. She was laid back on her recliner, looking at the television, trying to figure out the puzzle. I knew it, and I wanted to help her, but she always got mad when I told her the answer. She struggled for a minute more. Then, she finally blurted out the answer.

"The Empire State Building!" she screamed as she looked back and noticed that I was standing there.

Uncle Red's pissy ass was still snoring up a storm on the couch. I liked when she was in a good mood. I didn't know if I should ask her if I could hang with Peanut at the club.

So, I asked, "Can I go over to Kimmy's for a while?"

She looked at me and said, "I guess you can go over there for a few hours."

It was the weekend, and I wanted to get out of the house. I wanted to, at least, wear something fly over to Kimmy's house. Granny walked me to the door, and, as I walked out, she said, "Don't get in any shit."

"I'm not, and I love you, Granny," I said as I headed to Kimmy's house.

I knew that Granny would watch me until she couldn't see me anymore. So, I walked in the direction of Kimmy's house. Then, I looked back and saw that Granny had closed the door. I bypassed Kimmy's building and went to Peanut's apartment. I was going to Kimmy's, but I wasn't going to go just yet.

When I got to Peanut's apartment, Speedy was outside washing Peanut's car. He had the music playing loud, so I beat on the rails as I ran up the steps to the door.

"What's up? It's me. Black," I said as I pressed my head against the burglar bar door.

Peanut came to the door and locked it behind me.

"I thought your granny wasn't never going to let you back out."

"Man, that's just how my overprotected granny acts."

"I can't blame her, though. I wish I'd had somebody to go across my head," Peanut said as he put his keys on the coffee table. "You're one of the lucky ones. Now, all you have to do is make it out of this damn hood alive."

"Did you hear those fools out there shooting earlier?"

"Yes."

"Who was it?" I asked as I sat back on the sofa.

"It was that stupid-ass nigga Scooter, shooting at a junkie for trying to run off with a dime bag."

"Now, that's crazy!"

"Man, shit is getting crazy around these Bricks," Peanut said as he fired up a blunt. "I don't know about the rest of these niggas around here, but I am tired of selling this crack, rock, and powder shit. I really want to get out of the hood. I want to live like these niggas that I see on the TV. They are in their mansions, pouring thousands of dollars worth of champagnes, and driving the best cars. I mean, I do alright, but I want to move on. For example, I have a few hundred thousand dollars, but I can't go out and buy a house. Who do you know will sell a nigga like me a house? I have a mouthful of gold teeth, and I have these tattoos everywhere. I don't know what made me get these damn tattoos on my face. I guess I was just going ink crazy. But back to your granny, though.

I can tell that that little old lady loves you. She's not going to let anything happen to you if she can help it. And I can't blame her. I wish I had my grandma, or, hell, I would even take my mama with her strung out ass. It's a damn shame how all of us lost, young black men have to fend for ourselves. Shit is fucked up out here in these cold-blooded streets. The whole world is crazy. Everybody is killing each other, and no one seems to have love for one another. I don't mean to sound like a bitch or anything, but I do think about life and shit. I wonder where my mama is and if she is dead or alive. I wonder if that crack has blown her heart up yet.

Enough about all of that. What do you want to get into tonight? I am starting to feel like I am a lost, lonely-ass bitch. Here I am, the hardest nigga in the hood, bitching up, telling you my problems and shit."

"We all have problems," I said as I reached for the blunt. "It's okay to think about life. It's okay to express your feelings, too. You're not alone. I wonder where Priscilla is, too. I feel your pain because we didn't ask to be here. But my granny has always told me that it's not where you come from, it's where you're going. My granny has always told me to tell her my problems, whether I thought that she wanted to hear them or not. She has always said that I could be a ticking time bomb that's getting ready to explode or I could be a walking testimony who could help the next person. I've always listened to her because she has never steered me wrong."

"Well, at least, you have someone that loves you. And not only does she love you, she shows it, too."

We both dapped it up and smoked a few more blunts. We sat there on the sofa, high as hell. Then, he jumped up and said, "Let's get fresh and hit the club. You know where your room is," he said as we both headed to the back.

I went to the back room and looked at all of my clothes that were lined up. As I walked towards the window, I looked at Kimmy's building. I saw her sitting on her porch. Then, I looked through the closet and grabbed a True Religion outfit.

"Feel free to take a shower," Peanut said as he peeped in on me.

As I walked out of the room and headed to the bathroom, I saw what appeared to be a bag with the clothes in it. The closer I got, the more I noticed that they were the clothes that I'd had on the night that I shot Trevino. *He said he would burned them*, I thought. I scratched the top of my head and mumbled, "These *are* the clothes that I had on that night. What's up with this?"

The blood had dried up, and they had a foul smell. I closed them tightly in the bag and headed to the bathroom to take a shower. I turned on the hot water. Then, I turned on the cold water and adjusted it to my liking. The water in the Bricks was always scolding hot. And, if you didn't check it before getting in, you'd probably get third degree burns.

I let the water run down my face and all over my body. I stood in there, thinking, Why *in the hell hasn't Peanut burned those bloody clothes yet?* I was definitely going to ask him before the night was over.

The shower and the hot steam felt so good on my body. I wrapped a towel around me and went back to the bedroom. I saw a girl out of the corner of my eye. She was in Peanut's room.

"Knock! Knock!" I heard a girl's voice say as I sat on the bed. "I can dry you off," she said as she opened the door and walked on in.

"I'm good," I said, holding the towel around me.

"What's wrong with you? Are you scared of pussy?" she asked as she sat next to me on the bed.

"No, it's not that, and I don't want it if it's that easy."

"Well, what is it then?" she asked as she eased next to me.

"I have a girl, and I don't cheat on her."

"Well, suit yourself," she said as she walked out the room with an attitude.

And to make matters worse, she was smelled like fish. She was looking good in that short-ass dress that she had on, but she wasn't easy on the face. So, I was glad that I passed that up. I got up and locked the door because I didn't want any more strange pussy walking in throwing itself at me.

When I got up to lock the door, I noticed that the bag of clothes was gone from behind the door. *Maybe, he decided to burn them after all,* I thought as I put on my fly shit. *Let me see how it feels to be a rich nigga. These are the clothes that the rappers rap about.*

After getting spiffed up, I didn't feel any different. I was still the same black-ass nigga in the Bricks. I was super clean. I must admit. The Jordans set the True Religion outfit off perfectly. All I needed was a haircut. I had hair growing down the back of my neck, and that fucked up my whole outfit.

When I stepped in the living room where Peanut was, his company had already left.

"Now, you look like you should be hanging with me," Peanut said. "I see you turned Strawberry down," he said as he checked out my gear.

"Who was that anyway?"

"She's a powder head who thinks that she still looks good. She went from hot to not overnight. On the first night that she sniffed the soft for the very first time, the rest was history. She's been hooked ever since. See, that cocaine isn't for everybody. I mean, I bump every now and then, but I maintain."

"You mean to tell me that you do drugs?"

"Shit, yeah! That is one of the perks of this crazy-ass lifestyle that I live. See, watch," he said as he took a key and put it in a baggie and sniffed a white mini mountain off of the key. "Do you want to try it?"

"Hell, no!" I said quickly.

"Well, we definitely can't go to the club with your hair looking like it belongs to an extra on *Good Times*. I've already arranged for my boy Bobby's World to come over here and give you a hundred dollar haircut."

"One hundred dollars for a haircut?" I asked in disbelief.

"You mean to tell me that you've never heard of Bobby's World? He's the barber that is known for the hundred dollar haircuts and the million dollar swag. He's, also, known for cutting Ludacris's braids off."

"Now that you mention Ludacris, I think I sort of remember him now. It's coming back to me now. I, also, remember hearing a theme song that he made for his God-given skill. He, also, cut Gucci Mane, Shawty Lo and Soulja Boy's hair, too. He's a skilled barber, and he's known to all of the celebrities. This right here will show you everything," he said as he went to his HP Touch Smart computer. He pulled Bobby's World up on the internet.

"That's Gucci Mane right there," I said as I pointed at the computer. "And there goes Shawty Lo. Okay. Now, I see that he looks connected. Wow! Look at Shawty Lo's beard. That is a perfect line."

I was in shock. I was about to get my haircut by the man I had seen on the computer with some very high profiled celebrities.

"Yep, and that's why I don't let nobody but him touch my head," Peanut said as he opened the door for Bobby's World.

"What's up, Bobby? I was just telling my boy Black that you work miracles with your hands."

"That's right," he said as he walked in with a Gucci duffel bag.

Bobby walked in with a t-shirt on that had BOBBY'S WORLD written across the front of it. He was definitely a man about his business.

Bobby didn't talk too much as he put the cape around my neck and went to work. When he was done, I looked in the mirror and saw that I looked like a new nigga.

"Damn!" I said as I gave him a handshake. "What kind of haircut is this?" I asked as I stared at myself in the mirror. "And how did you make it so neat around the edges?"

"This is called a temp fade. I cut the edges with a razor."

"Wow! I didn't even know that I had enough hair on my face to have a goatee."

"That's all a part of my specialty—to make you look like a new you."

Then, he looked at Peanut and said, "As always, it's nice doing business with you."

After Peanut paid him, he gathered his things and left. "Now, you look like a grown-ass man."

"I do, don't I?" I said as I felt my face. I couldn't believe that I had facial hair. I only had a few strings, but I guess that was all he needed to work with. That Bobby had magical hands for real because I looked good.

"Here. Put this in your pocket," Peanut said as he threw me a stack of money.

This all seemed like a dream to me. And all I could think about was Granny coming to the club and beating my ass.

Chapter 10: *Somebody Pinch Me*

When we stepped outside of Peanut's apartment, it seemed like everyone had stopped what they were doing to focus their undivided attention on us. We were the center of attention. That was for sure. Peanut's Caprice was clean, and so were we. We both looked like a million bucks. Peanut had on a Versace shirt, of course. He said that he wanted people to know what he was wearing. And this Versace shirt had a unique design on the front of it. He had on a pair of Versace shades. He had even given me a pair of his pricey shades. I couldn't even pronounce the name of them. So, I just put them on. When I did, I felt like I was a rapper for real.

I walked down the steps slowly, letting everyone see a nigga that had transformed in only a matter of hours. Peanut took his chrome pistol out of his pants and sat it in his lap. I looked at the black handle gun. Then, I looked at him.

He said, "This is my best friend through thick and thin. God isn't the only one who won't leave you nor forsaken you. This Glock Nineteen is just as loyal."

He picked it up and kissed the handle of the gun.

"I respect that," I said as I unknowingly reached for my seat belt. When I realized what I was doing, I quickly let the strap go.

"You can ride with that strap around you if you want to. I just don't roll like that," Peanut said as he put the car in reverse.

"I'm cool," I said as I sat back. "Can we make one stop before we go to the club?"

"I know you don't want to stop by your house."

"You got jokes," I said as I looked at a girl walking her baby in a stroller in front of us.

"Bitch! Get out of the street," Peanut screamed as he turned the radio down. "You're old news," he said as he honked the horn at her.

"Fuck you!" she shouted back.

"I want to stop by Kimmy's house."

"You're talking about that smart, little, thick red bone that stays in the back?"

"Yeah. That's her."

"Yeah, we can stop by there. Are you hitting that?" Peanut asked as he looked over at me.

"Hell, yeah, and I am hitting it from all kinds of angles, too."

"Are you hitting that mouth, too? Remember what I told you. You have to have a different bitch for all of your needs."

"Nah. I am cool with just one girl."

"Oh! So, you're saying that you're a one woman man? Fuck that. Not me. I am hitting everything that moves. But you got yourself a good girl. I tried to fuck her, and she didn't budge," he said nonchalantly. "I wouldn't be a real nigga if I didn't try to hit that. Hell! I tried her mama, too, and both of them didn't give in. So, I guess you're the lucky nigga that she's been saving that pussy for."

"I guess you could say that," I said as I got out of the car and headed to Kimmy's door.

Peanut didn't know or care if I had feelings for Kimmy or not. He spoke his mind, and it didn't matter what the situation was. He was just a direct-ass nigga. But I was more of an observer. I was like a lion in the jungle. I just sat back and watched. Then, when the coast was clear, I would go in for the kill. Kimmy's mama was away at work. I knocked on the door, and she looked surprised to see me when she opened the door.

"I wouldn't have recognized you if it wasn't for that smile of yours, looking like Lance Gross. Whose clothes are you wearing?" she said as she peeped out and saw Peanut's car.

She pulled me into the house and said, "Please tell me that you are not selling drugs for that loser."

"I am not selling drugs for that loser," I repeated.

"Well, how did you get this True Religion that you're wearing?"

"Can I get a kiss?" I asked as I grabbed her hand. "What's with the thousand questions? Peanut is just looking out for me because he says that I remind him of himself."

"Huh? What kind of sense does that make?"

"Kimmy, please trust me and believe me when I say that I am not caught up in any drugs."

"But he sells drugs, and what if he has some in the car and y'all get pulled over by the police?"

"Baby, please stop thinking negative. Think positive, okay?"

Black, I care for you, and I don't want you to get caught up with these no good-ass niggas in the hood. And how did you get a beard? I knew you had a little facial hair, but now you look like a grown-ass man."

"Yeah. This is a little something new that Peanut

hooked me up with."

"Demetrius, swear to me that you are not selling drugs."

"I swear to you that I am not selling any drugs. Peanut hooked me up with a barber who knows all the stars."

"You're talking about Bobby?"

"Yeah. How do you know?"

"Everyone knows Bobby. He's the one who cut Luda's braids off. He hooked you up, too," she said as she checked my haircut out.

"I wanted to stop by here because I wanted to see you before I went to the club, and I, also, will need an alibi for Granny."

"Black, why are you going to the club with Peanut? Everybody knows that he's up to no good. And what about your granny? Does she know that you're hanging with him?"

"Well, not exactly," I stuttered. "I told her that I would be around here with you. So if you hear a knock at the door, don't answer it. It's a little after ten o'clock now, and she'll probably come around here looking for me. Baby, please just do this for me? You can pretend that we were asleep or something when we see her tomorrow."

"That's cool, but can you spend the night with me after the club because my mama is spending the weekend at her boyfriend's house? So, that alibi will work perfect," she said as she hugged me.

"Cool. That will work," I said as I kissed her and grabbed her ass. She walked me out to her porch. When she looked at Peanut, she rolled her eyes at him.

"Awww. That is so sweet," Peanut joked as I got back in the car. "We're going to see some pussy," Peanut said as we drove off. "We're going to the Blue Flame."

"What's the Blue Flame?"

"You'll see what it is in about five minutes. Black, you

got to know your own hood. It's a damn shame that all you know is the church and the corner store. Your granny has to stop sheltering you and let you get out more. You're on your way to manhood. You're about to graduate, and, after that, it is nothing but the real world."

When we pulled up at the Blue Flame, it was obvious that everyone already knew who he was, including security.

"They know me up here," he said as he whipped in the parking lot and hollered at Zay the AK . Zay the AK was the head of security. He was a big nigga with dreads, and he looked like he didn't take no shit either.

"Where do you want me to park?" Peanut asked.

"You can park by Antoinette's car."

We parked beside a white Charger that had the words STRAIGHT TO THE POINT BOOKS.COM magnetized on both sides.

"The girl who drives this Charger be at damn near every spot I go to, selling her books. Her name is Antoinette, and she has written a lot of books already. Wait until we walk up. We don't even have to say anything to her. She's going to approach us with those damn books."

"Hey, Peanut," Antoinette said as we got out of the car.

"What's up, Antoinette? I see you still hustling those books."

"I stay hustling my books, and, by the way, I have a new one out now. I don't have a choice but to sell my books because I got five kids by five pussy-ass niggas."

"Well, maybe, you should write a book about them since they're a bunch of losers."

"I wouldn't waste my ink on them bastards."

"Oh, okay. I feel you. So, how many does this make now?" Peanut asked as he went in his pocket to get some money out.

"This makes four books," she said as she came closer with her books in her hand for us to see. "Here's *Daddy's Favorite Pop; Married, Sneaky Black Woman; White Cop, Lil' Black Girl*, and *I'm a Drag, Not a Fag*."

"Wait a minute! What the hell is *I'm a Drag, Not a...*what? I don't know about that fag shit. But I will support you, so I will buy it. I might not never read it, but I will buy it."

"I respect that," Antoinette said as she autographed Peanut's books.

"I have those two already," Peanut said as he looked at *Daddy's Favorite Pop* and *Married, Sneaky Black Woman*.

"Okay. That's cool. Well, you can get these two for thirty bucks. What about you?" she said as she looked me up and down. "Why are you staring at me like that?" she asked.

"I never saw an author in real life selling their own books before."

"Oh, yeah? I get that a lot, but I am a realest. I don't plan on working for the white man ever again... or the black man, for that matter! I'm building my own empire from the ground up. I have five kids and two grandbabies. And I will write us out of the ghetto."

"You don't look like you live in the ghetto. You look pretty damn good to me."

"Are you trying to flirt with me? Not to mention, you look like you're my son's age. But we won't get into all of that. And speaking of my son, his name is Z3hree, and he will be performing his hit 'Rubberbands' tonight in the Blue Flame, so please stick around and watch him do his thing. And my mama Iwanna is here with me tonight. She is visiting from Texas, and she came to see her grandson Z3hree perform. Do you see her over there with that pink and white Straight to the Point Books T-shirt on?"

"Yeah, I see her," Peanut said. "You two could go for

sisters. You look just like her."

"Everybody tells us that when we go clubbing together. Hell! She's only fourteen years older than me. So, anyway I have a daughter. Her name is Driah, and she's about to have a little girl in July, and she will start working on her singing career once she drop that load. All of my kids will be somebody that's doing something to put some money in their pocket. And not to mention my last two boys Chicken and Fat Boy."

"Hold up!" Peanut said. "Why in the hell did you name those boys Chicken and Fat Boy?"

"They're just nick names. Their real names are Atiba and Khalil. Chicken is the next Michael Vick or Ray Allen because he has an arm that is out of this world, and he can hoop in basketball, too. And Fat Boy is a good running back, but he is, also, another Kevin Hart. He is so silly, and he makes me laugh everyday when he gets home from school."

I decided to stop her because she was not going to stop talking about her kids.

"Let me see your books. I read, too," I said as I reached for her books.

I quickly glanced at the back cover and the inside of the book.

"I see this list of your upcoming books. What will *Blackout on Bankhead* be about?"

"It's going to be about every black man's struggle, which is living in the hood and trying to make it out alive. I'm telling it from the perspective of a young black boy who lives with his granny in the hood. I talk about how he gets caught up in the street life."

"Damn! That sounds just like me. You need to hurry up with that one. I most definitely want to read that one."

"It will be out very soon, and, if you see that Charger right there, don't hesitate to flag me down," she said as she pointed at her car.

"You need to give me some of that money you've been making. I know that you have made, at least, one million dollars," Peanut said.

"If I'd made a million dollars, I wouldn't be out grinding as hard as I do."

"Well, you need to put me in your next book. I got a *New York Times* Bestseller for your ass. Or you could write my book for me."

"I don't ghostwrite, but my editor Windy does. I could hook you two up."

"That's even better," Peanut said as he walked away.

"I will take all four of them," I said as I handed them back for her to autograph them. "You can put my real name in there," I said as I began to spell out my name. "It's D-e..."

"What's your name?" she asked, cutting me off.

"It's Demetrius. I can spell that. I am a writer, and I can pretty much spell anything. That will be sixty dollars for all four."

"Here's one hundred dollars, and you can keep the change. I respect what you're doing. Keep up the good work," I said as I headed to put the books in the car.

"That's so sweet of you," she said as she went back to the long line of eager readers to get her hustle on.

We sat in the car for a moment, and Peanut said, "We might, also, go to Club Crucial and see Tripp James perform his song 'Dick Monkey'. He was born in Bankhead Courts, but he was raised in Bowen Homes."

"I don't mind going to see this nigga rap his life story."

I had never been to a club before in my life. This was something all new to me. I saw everyone wearing all of the latest trends. But no one was rocking what we were rocking. Peanut walked over to Zay the AK and paid him the cost for us parking in VIP.

"Let's go in here and get wasted," he said as he looked at the long line of people waiting.

He had done just how he did when we went to Georgia Power. He had no respect for the people who were standing in line. I followed him, and he paid for us to get in. As soon as we walked in, there were naked women everywhere. And when we walked in, Antoinette's son Z3hree was on the stage, and he had the whole club going wild. That song "Rubberbands" was a strip club banger. But the more I looked at the naked women, the more I felt like I was about to get a hard on, but I had to have dick control. I didn't want to look like a horny, shocked dog in a strip club. *So, this is the Blue Flame,* I thought as I looked at all the money that covered the floor. There were people throwing money everywhere, including women. And I was shocked because the women who were throwing the money were pretty women, too.

"This is what I'm talking about," Peanut said as we headed to the VIP area. "Look at all these fine-ass bitches in here," he said as he threw a bundle of ones before sitting down.

I wanted to throw some money, too, but I only had a stack of twenties. I grabbed a handful and threw them in the air. That immediate caught the attention of one of the dancers. She came over to where we were.

"What's up, Peanut?" she said as she sat on the sofa in between us.

"You know how I do it when I come in here," Peanut said as he waved for Kelly to bring us a bottle of champagne.

Kandee brought us some hot wings, but it wasn't enough for all of that alcohol that we had consumed.

"Look at Lita's fine ass, on stage, making all that cash," Peanut said.

"Who is your new friend?" the dancer asked Peanut as

if I was a mute.

"You can ask me who I am," I said as I looked at the stage.

"Well, then, who are you?" she asked as she stood up in front of me.

"My name is Black."

"Black," she repeated. "Your mama didn't name you Black, so what's your real name?"

"My real name is Demetrius, but all of my friends and my granny call me Black."

"That nickname fits you because you're one sexy, black-ass nigga." She stood there and began to make her ass clap. "Do you like what you see?" She turned around and opened her legs wide open. She had tattoos all over her body, and she was fine, just like Kimmy.

"Hell, yeah! I like what I see. What's your name?" I asked as I tried to read some of her body ink.

"You can call me whatever you want to call me," she said as she dipped down to the floor.

"I want to call you Fluffy since your ass is bouncing lightly as you shake your legs."

"Sounds good to me," she said as she sat in my lap and grinded up and down on my dick.

Now, my dick was getting hard for sure, and there was no way I could make it go down. She was grinding on me like we were fucking. I felt like I was about to cum in my jeans.

"I can feel your third leg," she said as she kneeled over and continued dancing.

Then, I was saved by the bell when Peanut came over and told her that she was relieved of her duties. He gave her a one hundred dollar bill. She hugged Peanut and told him thanks. Then, she winked at me and kissed me on my neck as she left. Peanut called Drake the picture man over. After all was said and done, we must have taken, at least, two hundred dollars worth of pictures.

"So, this is how the ballers hang, huh?"

"You're exactly right," Peanut said as he showed a gold bottle of champagne. It looked like it was made with real twenty-four karat gold. "Look around you. We're the only motherfuckers in here with this good shit. This is Jay Z's shit! This is the best champagne on the market. It's called Ace of Spades, and it's supposed to be sipped by a made-ass nigga, such as myself."

He poured us a glass, and I sipped as I looked at all of the beautiful, naked women. The music was loud, and it had eventually faded Peanut's voice out as he tried to talk to me. He ordered another bottle, and it was vodka. We were definitely the center of attention because he was throwing money, and I was throwing money. It blew my mind, how the girls were shaking their asses. Their bodies were oiled up, and they were built like stallions. We sat in there and drank and smoked and had a good time. I looked at everyone else, and everybody was having fun, too. I could have sworn that I saw Shawty Lo in there, but I didn't want to look like a stan. This felt like a dream to me, and I was just sitting there, waiting for someone to pinch me and wake me up. Peanut hugged the owner of the Blue Flame, Ms. Jackie, and we left.

By the time we left, we both were drunk as hell. I didn't see how Uncle Red drank all that alcohol. My throat, along with my insides, felt like they were on fire. We got in the car, and Peanut changed the CD.

"Man, we got to go to Church's Chicken, so we can put some more grease on our stomachs to soak up all that damn alcohol we drank," Peanut said.

I let the seat back and laid back because my head was spinning.

"I knew we should have gotten a fifty piece wing while we were in the club," Peanut said. "How do you feel, Black Boy?"

"I feel like my Uncle Red, and I see why he sleeps so hard. I feel like I am about to pass out."

"You'll feel better as soon as we go down here to this chicken house. Big Henry always has that fresh bird, and I could use two wings and three legs right about now."

"And you can't forget about the peppers," I added.

"Hell, yeah! My mouth is watering now," he said as he pressed his foot on the gas pedal.

When we pulled up at Church's, he parked sideways, taking up two parking spaces, and left the music was blasting. It felt like we were still in the club.

"Come on, Black Boy. I want to introduce you to these good people in here."

"Welcome to Church's," a lady said as we entered.

"What's up, Foxy? Where's Big Henry?" Peanut asked.

She called Big Henry to the front.

"Order what you want, fool, and get me the same thing." Then, he looked at Foxy and said, "Are you ready to give me those digits yet?"

"Boy, please," she said, brushing him off.

"I'm dead-ass serious," Peanut said as he leaned on the counter. "You know I like my women thick, and I been trying to get at you for a long time now."

"Peanut, I have told you a million times that you're too young for me," Foxy said.

"Is that the real reason, or are you scared of this?" he said as he slammed a wad of money on the counter.

Big Henry looked over and said, "Man, you better put that money up. You're on Bankhead."

"I know where I'm at. Hell! I was born and raised in the

Bricks. Besides, I got the heat right here," he said as he lifted up his shirt.

"Okay. Then, you're the boss," Henry said as he packed our food, and we left.

Chapter 11: *My Girl Kimmy*

When we got back to the Bricks, I was still feeling the effects of the vodka. The chicken did a little justice but not much. We both sat in the car and talked until the sun came up. I had already lost count of the blunts that we had smoked. I knew that Granny was probably worried sick about me, but, if Kimmy did what I had told her to do, then everything would be alright.

We sat in the car until we heard the birds chirping. For some reason, that night reminded me of the night when we had buried Trevino. The atmosphere was the same. The night air was so crisp and foggy. I thought about his murder from time to time, but, like Peanut had said, "Little niggas get killed every day." I knew, for a fact, that we couldn't roam this earth forever, so I had come to believe that Trevino had it coming. He had put himself in that situation and sped up his own demise. He had cut his own life short by trying to rob the hood's craziest drug dealer. We sat in the car and listened to T.I's new CD *Trouble Man*. I felt like I was a trouble man who hadn't gotten in any trouble yet.

"Do you want to come upstairs and stay with me, or do

you want to go back to your granny's this early in the morning?"

"I have a better plan. I am going to Kimmy's. We already have our alibi together for my granny."

"Alright. Cool," Peanut said as he drove off.

When we pulled up in front of Kimmy's building, I got out the car and walked around to Kimmy's window. She looked out and came to open the door.

"Did my granny come by?" I asked as I walked in.

"No. No one came by," she said as she locked the door.

"Good," I said as I fell across her bed.

"You smell like a walking liquor bottle," she said as she took off my shoes. "But you're still my baby."

She took off my Jordans and put them in the corner.

"Come here," I said as I made room for her to cuddle with me in the bed.

"Aren't you going to take your clothes off?" she asked as she started to take off my jeans.

"I can do it," I said as I jumped up and quickly fell to the floor. "I am drunk as hell," I said as I felt like I was about to throw up.

"You shouldn't have drunk alcohol anyway," she said as she kneeled down with me on the floor.

"It's too late now. I am drunk as hell, so can you please help me get out of these jeans?"

She helped me get back on the bed and take my jeans off.

"Now, hold your arms up, so I can help you out of this shirt. Now, that's better," she said as she neatly folded my clothes and put them on her dresser.

"I feel better already," I said as I felt her warm body next to mine.

When I woke up the next day, it was dark.

"What time is it?" I asked as I stretched my arms to the

ceiling. Kimmy was in the mirror combing her hair.

"It's seven thirty, and you have been sleeping for hours. I mean, what did you expect you got here at seven in the morning? I didn't want to disturb you. Plus, you needed to sleep that alcohol off."

"Did my granny come by yet?"

"No, she didn't."

I got up and put on my clothes.

"I feel like a new nigga. Now, I see why Uncle Red sleeps all day after he's been drunk."

At least, I didn't piss on myself, I thought as I put on my shoes.

"I will be back in a few."

"I'm coming with you," Kimmy said as she grabbed her coat and locked up.

"We have to make one stop first. We have to stop by Peanut's apartment, so I can change clothes. My granny will kill me if she sees me in these high priced clothes."

"I'm not going to Peanut's apartment. I will stay at the bottom of the steps."

"Girl, will you stop acting like that. You're with me, and I'm not going to let anything happen to you. You said, you want us to be together forever, right?"

"Right," she said as she grabbed my hand and headed with me up the stairs to Peanut's apartment.

I used my keys and let myself in.

"You can't be serious. You have keys to his apartment, too."

"Yo!" I said as I walked in to let Peanut know that I wasn't an intruder.

"His car wasn't downstairs," Kimmy said, "so he's probably not here."

She looked around and noticed the flat screen TVs that were on the wall.

"Can we please hurry up and get out of here? I don't want to be in here."

She followed me to my bedroom that was all the way in the back. Her eyes grew big as she looked at all the nice clothes and shoes that Peanut had bought me.

"Are all of these your clothes?" she asked as she fiddled through the price tags. "What are you doing for him to buy you all of these expensive-ass clothes?"

"I did him a small favor, and he showed his token of appreciation this way."

I put back on my dingy-ass, wrinkled clothes, and we locked up and headed to Granny's house.

"We're not done talking about why he *really* bought you all of those expensive clothes."

"Will you just drop it?" I said as I grabbed her hand.

"I am not about to have a drug dealer for a boyfriend."

"I told you that I am not a drug dealer."

As we approached my building, there was an ambulance parked out front. Kimmy and I ran to my door and found that my granny was on a stretcher. The paramedics were bringing her out the front door. Her eyes were closed, and she had an oxygen mask on her face.

"What the fuck happened to my granny?" I shouted.

Chapter 12: *My Praying Grandmother*

"Sir, I will need for you to calm down," one of the paramedics said.

"You calm the fuck down and tell me what the fuck happened to my granny! Granny, wake up! It's me. Demetrius. Granny, please don't leave me. I'm sorry for not coming home last night. Please wake up and talk to me, granny."

I was crying like I had lost my best friend. My granny was my everything. She was my rock.

"Sir, we got a call from her saying that she was having numbness on one side of her body. We're not doctors, so we're not at liberty to give any type of diagnosis, but you can ride with us to Grady Memorial Hospital, if you'd like. But I will need for you to calm down."

I watched them as they put my granny in the ambulance.

"I'm coming, too," Kimmy said.

"Ma'am, there's only enough room for one person to ride along, and we prefer for it to be family."

I heard a horn honking, and it was Peanut. I was relieved because I wanted Kimmy to be by my side. We walked over to Peanut's car, and we both got in.

Before we left, I said, "I have to go and lock up," as I got my keys out of my pocket.

Kimmy got out of the car and followed me. I went in the living room and shook Uncle Red to ask him what happened to my granny, but he wouldn't wake up. I went to the refrigerator and grabbed a milk jug of cold water and poured it over his head.

"Wake up, Uncle Red! My granny is on the way to the hospital."

"What?" he said as he shook the water from his face.

"You heard me. My granny is on the way to the hospital. You mean to tell me that you was asleep when all those white folks was in here?"

"What white folks?"

"The damn ambulance people! If I stay here any longer and try to talk some sense into you, it's only going to piss me off, and I will hurt you."

"Wait a minute!" he said as he stood up. "I'm coming, too," he said as he staggered to the front door.

As we were walking out of the door, Priscilla was walking in. She was the last person that I wanted to see.

"Mama has been rushed to the hospital," Uncle Red said to Priscilla.

"She's being what?" Priscilla asked as she began to weep on the steps.

"Let's all go," Peanut shouted as we stood there in a panic.

We all gathered in Peanut's car. I got in the front seat, and they got in the back. He turned the music down and said, "It's a family affair."

I knew he knew that Priscilla was on drugs, and I knew he had sold to her before. It was so awkward. Peanut rolled a blunt, and, of all people, Priscilla asked if she could hit it. Peanut looked at me and said, "Is it cool for me to pass your mama the blunt?"

"My *mama* is on her way to Grady," I said as I looked at Priscilla, who was reaching for the blunt.

I looked back at Kimmy, and she had her hand over her face to cover the weed smoke.

"You might as well pass it to me," Uncle Red said.

Peanut said, "It's cool. I got plenty more where that came from."

When we arrived at Grady, I rushed out of the car, and Kimmy followed closely behind.

"I need to see my granny," I said as I approached the information booth.

"What's the name of the patient?"

"Never mind her name. She was brought in here by ambulance."

"Sir, people get brought in here by the ambulance all day every day."

"Her name is Mattie Lee Smith," Priscilla said as she arrived at the information booth.

"I found her," the receptionist said. "It looks like she's at the Marcus Stroke and Neuroscience Center."

We all rushed to where my granny was. When we got in the room, she was laying in the hospital bed, motionless.

The doctor walked in and said, "Ms. Smith has had a stroke."

"What does that mean? Is my granny going to die?"

"Let me explain it to you, son. A stroke is a sudden interruption of the blood supply in the brain. Ms. Mattie has suffered an ischemic stroke. We did an MRI, and we found a blood clot on the left side of her brain. It doesn't mean that she's going to die. She could have numbness on one side if she wakes up from this deep coma that she's in. These types of strokes are common in elderly patients. Plus, she has high blood pressure."

"What does that mean? Is she going to die or not? She has so many pills around the house. How did this happen?"

"These things happen to us because some of us are stressed and some of us just have a poor diet. But, right now, there is very little brain activity, and we can't operate because Ms. Mattie has been a patient of mine for over thirty years, and she signed a paper saying that she wouldn't want surgery in the event that something like this should ever happen."

"Well, at least, she has life insurance, and I am the beneficiary," Priscilla said.

"Really, Priscilla? My granny is probably on her death bed, and all you can think about is a life insurance policy."

"No. I'm the beneficiary," Uncle Red said.

"I can't believe you two stupid stooges. Do either one of you care that my granny might die?"

The doctor looked at me and said, "I know this is hard for you, but you have to start thinking about memorial plans. She does not look good, and it will be a miracle if she comes through."

Uncle Red and Priscilla had already left the room. They were standing in the hallway.

"I know how you feel," Kimmy said.

I looked at her. Then, I looked at my granny. I stood over my granny and prayed. I prayed how she had taught me to pray ever since I was a little boy. I looked at my granny and said, "I know that you can hear me. I need for you to fight. This isn't in God's plan. You even said it yourself that, when I graduate, you're going to jump for joy and be so happy. My graduation isn't for five more months. God, please don't let my granny die. She's all that I have. What will happen to me, God? Where will I go? Where will I live? Who will cook that good soul food that my granny cooks? Who will pray for me? This is my praying grandmother, and I need her right now. God, please hear me. I need my granny!"

Peanut walked in and said, "Be strong, Black Boy. I know what you're going through. I got to head back to the Bricks. Are you coming?"

"No, I'm not coming, I'm not leaving my granny's side. I will be right here when she opens her eyes."

"Are you coming, Kimmy?" he asked.

"No, I'm staying right here with Demetrius."

"Okay. Cool. Call my Metro when you need me."

He left and Priscilla and Uncle Red rode back with him to the Bricks. It was winter break, and we were out of school for two weeks. I was not going to leave my granny's side. She was a strong little lady, and I knew she would pull through. Kimmy started talking about her daddy. I didn't want to hear about her daddy. Some people should know when not to take other people's moment. But I guess she was trying to sympathize with me. But she wasn't helping at all. Her daddy had already died, and my granny was still breathing.

Chapter 13: *I Love My Granny*

A week had gone by, and there were no changes in my granny's situation. Kimmy's mother had come and gotten her, and it was just me and my granny all alone. Kimmy stayed as long as she could, but we both knew that it would be only a matter of time before her mother would come to pick her up.

Uncle Red and Priscilla hadn't even been back to the hospital to check on their own mother. They were the ones who should have had a fucking stroke and died! The nurses and the doctors did the same shit every day. They came in and took my granny's vitals. They lifted up her eyelids and saw that her pupils were dilating. And that was a good sign of life. *I will never give up on my granny because my granny has never given up on me,* I thought over and over. Even though she was breathing with the help of a ventilator, she was taking in forty percent of that oxygen on her own. I held her hand as it rose up and down on her stomach. I hated that there was nothing that I could do for her. I remember when my granny used to walk me home from school, and she would tell me to look up at the sky. Then, she would ask me to reach for the sky. But I could never reach the sky because it was so far away, and she would always say that the sky is the limit. She let me know that, whatever I wanted to do or become in life, I could.

She said, "Look at Barack Obama. He's part African, and he was raised by his grandmother. And look at him now. He is the president of the United States."

I can just sit back and think about all the stuff that my granny used to tell me to keep my black ass out of trouble. I watched the nurses as they checked my granny, and she was in the same condition. I really wish that there was something that I could do. I didn't really understand why my granny didn't want to have surgery, but I was glad that she had some sign of life in her eyes. And my granny had always told me that the eyes never lie. So, I had reason to believe that my granny would come back to me. I had about another week until winter break was over, and I did not want to leave my granny's side. But she wouldn't have it any other way. This was my last year in school, and I had to graduate and become the man that my granny wanted me to be.

I was sitting in the chair, watching the daily news, and saw that there was always a killing in Atlanta. It didn't matter if it was in the city part or the country part. Somebody, somewhere, was taking his last breath of life.

I do not want to make the statistics list. I am seventeen, and I plan on making it to see twenty-one years of age, I thought.

Peanut had come by the hospital to pick me up and take me to the Bricks to bathe. Uncle Red and Priscilla were there, drinking and smoking crack, as usual. Those two seriously needed help. Their mother was in the hospital, and they were carrying on like they didn't have a care in the world. When I walked in, Priscilla was reading over Granny's life insurance policy, and she said, "See, Red. I told you that I am the beneficiary."

I had never raised a hand at Priscilla before in my life, but she was asking for it. The thought of her thinking about insurance money at a time like this let me further know that she was a cold-hearted person. I walked past the two stupid dogs and went to my room. I laid across my bed and reminisced about the good times that I had had with my granny. There was never a dull moment. I had my video games, and I had my granny in the living room, watching *Wheel of Fortune*. There were times when Priscilla and Uncle Red were missing in action for a long time. And those usually were the times when the lights stayed on. Or those were the times when I didn't have to worry about sleeping in a pissy bed that Uncle Red had urinated in. I had got all of my new clothes from Peanut's trap house, and I dared Priscilla or Uncle Red to touch them. I changed the lock on the bedroom door, and I had made it known to Uncle Red that the living room would be his bedroom from now on.

I hadn't thought much about the homicide, but guilt had started to sink in. I started to think about some of the things that Trevino said as far as not having a grandmother. He asked me what it was like to have a grandmother. I couldn't even come to grips. *What will my next move be if my granny died tomorrow? I will be shit out of luck. She's all that I know*, I thought. Priscilla had never stepped up to the plate, not even when I had to be rushed to the hospital for a high fever that I had. She never attended any of the parent-teacher meetings at school. She never attended any school plays that I participated in. She was just a poor excuse for the word mother. I was glad that she'd only had one child to take all of the mental abuse from her. I had to live with the fact that my biological mother was a crack head. Even though she'd been that way my whole life, I guess it was starting to sink in now that she really wasn't shit. All she cared about was getting high. I mean, there were nights when she would come home, looking like a zombie. She didn't even look like herself. She looked like something straight out of a horror movie. I had never disrespected her, but I didn't know how much more I could take of her trying to speed up my granny's death.

Chapter 14: *The Rundown*

I only had one more week before school started again, and Peanut had been trying to get me to go to Da Fox Phase 2. I was still shocked by all of the raw pussy that I had seen at the Blue Flame, but, as long as I was with Peanut, I knew that I was going to have a good time. I wasn't too fond of leaving my granny's side, but she had made some improvement. She was now breathing fifty percent on her own. I was extremely happy, and I wanted to be there as soon as my granny opened her eyes. The doctor had said that it was going to take a miracle, and, so far, the miracle was coming true. My granny had always believed in the Lord, and so had I because all I knew was the First Baptist Church. My granny made sure that I read out of my bible every night before I went to bed. I had scriptures memorized, such as Psalms 91 and John 3:16.

Peanut dropped me off back at Grady Memorial Hospital, and I stood over my granny, and I talked to her. I prayed for her. The nurse came in and said that I was such an obedient young man. And because of this, God would answer all of my prayers. Then, she whispered in my granny's ear and said, "You still have work to do here on earth."

She took my granny's vitals and left.

I sat in the chair and decided to take Peanut up on his offer and to go the club with him. He picked me up from the hospital, and he did his normal routine. He blasted his music and rolled a few blunts as he drove. He was actually driving and rolling up the blunt at the same time. He started to talk about all the clubs we could go to. I was about to put on my seat belt when I remembered that Gs didn't ride with seat belts. He passed me the blunt and said, "There is a lot of shit we can get into this weekend. We can go to a new club called Space. They don't close them doors until the last drunk motherfucker comes stumbling out. And that will be us, of course, because we will go there and put on for our city. I am going straight to the VIP area, and we will have, at least, five bottles of expensive alcohol."

As Peanut bragged about what we were going to do, I was trying not to hit the blunt too hard. But that was hard, considering that he had the best weed in Georgia. The weed was so strong that I only had to hit it a little and I was high as hell.

I mean, he had a spot for us to go to every single day of the week. He said, "On Monday, we are going to Magic City. On Tuesday, we will go to Club Rendezvous on Roosevelt Highway. It's been a minute since I saw my homeboy Dick. On Wednesday, we will go to Diamonds of Atlanta, where I never get enough of seeing those girls bust their pussies wide open." I had to give him a high five because I loved seeing sexy women of all races, dancing on the pole. He, also, said that local celebrities, like Gucci Mane and Gorilla Zoe, were known to hang in there. "On Thursday, we are going to the Blue Flame because we were so drunk last time that we didn't even get a chance to see Eyes slap those amateurs on the ass. On Friday, we're going to Da Fox on Bankhead. On Saturday, we will hit up Space, and, on Sunday, we will go to both of the Mexican bars on Old National Highway. We will go to El Nopal. It's owned by a cool-ass Mexican by the name of Escamilla J. Guadalupe. We will have a few drinks with Penguin. They have some good drinks, and Pablo, Aisha, Tony Montana or Horacio will hook us up. Then, we will finish our night in El Ranchero's VIP section and buy a few bottles from George and Nacho. But it gets crazy in there sometimes. When them niggas get drunk, I just sit back and laugh as Blu and his Dark Blue Security Team throw them out on their asses for being ignorant. His security team is a bunch of big-ass niggas. Rico, Biggs, Tee, and Dale are all some buff-ass niggas who don't take no shit in the El Ranchero Mexican Bar. And he told me to watch my ass when I go in there by myself because they throw skinny niggas out, too. Whenever I go to the El Ranchero, I always look for Daniel, Cheo, Antonio, Salvador, Alicia, Raqueim, or Paco to fix my drinks for me. They have the best food. We might go to the Velvet Room, too, but it depends on how drunk I get."

Peanut talked about these clubs like this was the only life that he'd known. But he did say that his life only consisted of making money, getting high, and fucking different girls. I only had one girl, and I was satisfied with her. She completed me in so many ways. She was always smiling when we were together. I really loved her, and I knew she got mad when she told me and I didn't tell her back. But, for some reason, I had to thank Priscilla for that. It was hard for me to show my girl love when I didn't even feel love from my own damn mama. I needed to stop thinking about Priscilla before she spoiled my whole week.

I wanted to stop by Kimmy's because it had been about a week since I had talked to her. Her mother was so serious about her going to college after high school. I didn't want to come between that because, from the looks of my life, I was going to be a street nigga. There was no way I could go to college. I wanted the fast cars and the wads of cash like Peanut had.

On our way to the Bricks, Peanut stopped in the flat land and pulled up on Adamsville Angie. She was sitting in an all white BMW 760. I couldn't help but to zoom my eyes to the white rims that stood out like snow. She stepped out, and she was dressed from head to toe. It was just something about the hood. It seemed that everybody had to be so fresh and so clean. She had on a pair of Robin's jeans, Burberry shoes, and the scarf to match. She was dressed for the unpredictable weather that Atlanta had to offer. She walked over to Peanut, and they shook hands, and then he introduced her to me.

"This is my boy Black," Peanut said as he passed her the blunt.

When she opened her mouth, I saw a gold grill that shined like a light bulb. She looked at Peanut's tires and said, "I see the meat on those tires. I told you, next time you want some tires, I can get them to you for the low low."

"Adamsville Angie, you got the hook up on everything," Peanut said as he passed the blunt to me. Peanut looked at her and said, "I know that you stay getting that money. You always have something going on. Next, you're going to tell me that you got the hook up on rims and cell phones and shit."

She looked at him and said, "Nigga, I got what you need from heroin to weed."

We all started laughing, and he told her that he would see her later, and we left.

"We have one more stop to make before we hit the Bricks. I gotta stop and check on something with my home girl named Big Sonia from Dixie Hills. Even though I fuck with a lot of bitches, I always have to have loyal bitches on my team."

All of that riding and smoking had made me tired. I wanted to just lay down in my twin bed and get some sleep. But I knew that it was probably pissy from Uncle Red's drunk ass. Going back and forth to the hospital with my granny and smoking with Peanut had really taken a toll on me. It seemed like, the more blunts we smoked, the more he rolled up. He was a functioning weed head who just happened to be a drug dealer.

When we arrived back at the Bricks, I did not want to go to my granny's house. But I knew, sooner or later, that I would have to face Uncle Red and Priscilla. We went to Peanut's apartment, and I took a quick shower and got fresh from head to toe. My clothes were still organized in the third bedroom's closet. I told Peanut that I was going to walk around to Kimmy's house. He told me to lock the burglar door as I left. When I walked down the steps, I felt like a boss man. Not only was I clean as fuck, I had keys to Peanut's apartment. Speedy walked over to me and said, "Let me get that for you."

"Get what for me?" I said.

"This," he said as he snatched the price tag out from the back of my True Religion shirt. "Good looking out," I said as I headed to Kimmy's house.

Chapter 15: *Power of Pussy*

When I knocked on Kimmy's door, she was shocked when she noticed the expensive clothes that I had on.

"Well, are you going to let me come in?" I said as I looked around and didn't notice her mother's car in the parking lot.

She opened the door, and we both headed to her bedroom. She got under her thick, fluffy pink comforter, and I sat on the edge of the bed. She, then, said, "Black, I am going to get straight to the point. If you're dealing drugs, I do not want to be around you — period."

"Girl, how many times do I have to tell you that I am not dealing any drugs."

"Well, why did Peanut buy you all of those expensive clothes?"

"Do we have to go through this again? I came over here because I missed you, and I wanted to see you before I go out to the club."

"The club?"

"Yes. The club."

She scooted down towards me on the bed and hugged me from behind and said, "Black, I love you with all of my heart. Please stay here with me tonight."

"I will be back after the club. By the way, where is your mother? Is she working overtime again?"

"She's always working overtime, and I go crazy when I am in this house all by myself."

"Why don't you read one of those books I bought you by that girl named Antoinette Smith?"

"Oh, my God! I meant to tell you about them. Her books were so good, definitely page turners, but that first one…*Daddy's Favorite Pop*…that book made me cry. And I was pissed off after I finished it, but, overall, it was an excellent book. Maybe, I need to hook up with her because I want to write about my life and about how I miss my daddy. But her books need to be made into movies. I can see them on the big screen. Her second book, *Married, Sneaky Black Woman*, was a good book. You should read that one. It was funny at times, but then it got serious all of the sudden. When I read her third book, *White Cop, Lil Black Girl*, I was so blown away. That book really had me on edge. She was so descriptive, and I visualized the whole book in my head. I mean, the way she wrote about the white cop seemed so real. He was a complete asshole in the book."

"Are you going to spoil it for me and tell me what they're all about, or can I find out for myself?"

"Okay. Let me just tell you about her fourth book called *I'm a Drag—*"

I cut her off because I didn't want to hear about any fag shit. It reminded me about when that fag had hit on me at Lenox Mall.

As I listened to Kimmy, I knew that she was lonely because she didn't hang with any girls in the Bricks. Most of them were jealous of her anyway because they were already having babies and half of them had to drop out of school.

She rubbed on me in all the right places. She knew that, once she kissed my ear, I wasn't going anywhere. That was my hot spot, and my dick was at attention in a matter of seconds. She was a freak, but that was okay because she was my freak. I knew that she wanted to fuck, but I wanted to hit up those clubs that Peanut was telling me about. But the power of pussy was right next to the power of prayer. And there was no way that I could turn that down. She helped herself to my jeans and unzipped them. She was sucking my dick through the zipper of my pants. I laid back on the bed, and I let her have her way. She was taking long licks and juggling my balls at the same time. My dick was rock hard, and I was ready to gain entry. I wanted to fuck her hard from the back, but she was sucking my dick so good that I busted a nut right in her mouth.

She cleaned me up, and I just laid there in a daze. She was a good girl, and I could tell, but I wanted to hang in the streets. It was calling my name. I mean, I had yet to feel what the street life was all about. Peanut made the streets look so good. He didn't have to worry about nothing. He had junkies watching out for him and selling drugs for him. I wanted that kind of rank. I wanted to know how it felt to be a boss man. As we both laid in the bed, she laid on my chest and said, "When are you going to eat my pussy?"

I was shocked because she was always the one damn near raping me. She had on a tank top and a pair of boy shorts, and her pussy print looked like it needed to be freed.

"Have you ever had somebody to go down on you before?"

"Boy, didn't I tell you that you were my first? I haven't had anything done to me. Have you ever ate pussy before?" she asked as she took off her boy shorts.

"Why do you say it so harsh? I mean, no, I haven't, so you will be my first and last. My Uncle Red has always told me not to eat something that could get up and walk away."

"Well, the only place I am walking is to school. Now, get over here and eat this pussy."

I didn't mind eating her pussy because she smelled of nothing but Palmer's Cocoa Butter lotion and strawberries. Her pussy was shaved low, and I didn't know where the hell to lick. So, I licked across the top. Then, I opened her pussy up and licked between her pussy lips. I must have been doing something right because she buried my head right there, and she moved it in a circular motion. I didn't even have control of my own head. She was moaning and screaming my name. Apparently, she had reached her peak, but she wasn't finished yet.

She straddled herself on top of my hard dick. Neither one of us mentioned any type of protection. She didn't say anything, and I didn't either. The warmth of her pussy sliding up and down my dick made a nigga go crazy. And it was sloppy wet because she had cum, and I felt her pussy juices gushing on my thighs. She was riding my dick like she was riding a bull. I rolled my head from side to side on the pillow. I was feeling a little weak, but I couldn't help it because she was a pro at making me feel good in the bed. I felt like my manhood was being tested in a sense because she was definitely manhandling me.

Chapter 16: *Truths*

Kimmy was something else when it came to sex. She knew all of the right moves, and she knew the exact words to say at the right time.

We took a scolding shower, and we both laid in the bed, talking about our future. She was focused on being a doctor, and I already knew that I was going to be the next Bricks dope boy. I heard what she was saying, but it was going in one ear and out of the other. My granny had spoken to me about my future until she was blue in the face, but I wouldn't stand a chance in college. I already hated going to school nine months out of a year. Because, for me, all it would take was for one person to clown me about my clothes, and I would be heading to the dean's office for fracturing a motherfucker's face.

As Kimmy laid on my chest, I thought about all of the fun that I would be missing if I had stayed the night with her. I'd had so much fun when we went out last time. It was still early and, as I listened to her, I had flashbacks of when those girls were stripping at the Blue Flame. Skittles, Luscious, Ambitious all danced around that pole like they owned it. And they even climbed all the way up the pole, then fell down hard, landing the perfect split. I had never seen anything like that in my life. Diamond didn't even do no shit like that in the Player's Club, and she was, by far, my favorite stripper.

I didn't want to leave that strip club. If I had my way, I would have stayed there all night long and watch them do pussy tricks. Kandee was a fine, thick-ass stallion, too. She was from Decatur, and she and Tracy worked in the kitchen in the Blue Flame, and they hooked those hot wings up. Kandee was fine as fuck, too, and she could go for a dancer, too. I couldn't get over how all those girls in there looked. Everywhere I looked, I saw eye candy, even the waitresses.

"Are you listening to me?" Kimmy asked as her voice faded back into my memory bank.

"Yeah, girl. I heard you. You said you want to be a doctor."

"Boy, your ass has been daydreaming. I said, 'Someone is at the door', and I want you to go answer it."

I got up and answered the door, and, to my surprise, it was Peanut.

"What's up?" he said as he tried to make his way through the door. "I see you're all over here, laid up and shit. It's time for us to hit the club."

By that time, Kimmy had walked in and said, "I thought that you were staying here with me tonight."

"Damn! Hold up! Are you pussy whipped already?" Peanut said as he looked at Kimmy.

I didn't know what to say. I didn't want to look like a punk in front of Peanut, so I said "Hell, no! I'm not pussy whipped."

I headed to Kimmy's room to put on my shirt and shoes. She was right behind me, saying, "You promised to stay the night with me."

I grabbed her hand and told her, "I am gonna spend the night with you, but, I am gonna hang out with Peanut first."

"But why do you have to hang with him out of all of the boys in the Bricks?"

"Because he's one of the realist niggas that I know."

"He's so real that he turned state's evidence on his own cousin."

"What are you talking about?" I asked as I sat on the edge of her bed.

"Have you seen Ray Ray around lately?"

She did have a point because I hadn't seen Ray Ray in a long time.

She continued, "The word around the Bricks is that he and Peanut were riding with some drugs and the police pulled them over. Well, at first, they both were going to claim the dope, but, when they interrogated them separately, Peanut decided to blame it all on Ray Ray, and he is now facing hard time. Demetrius, I don't want you to get into any trouble. It's so easy to get in. And, for some strange reason, I don't trust Peanut. He's the snake that you'd better watch."

"I can handle myself," I said as I put on my Atlanta Falcons fitted cap.

She hugged me so tight and kissed me. I knew that she loved me, and I had some love for her, too, but I had to be a man.

I went back into the front room where Peanut was and found him looking at Kimmy's pictures and trophies throughout her home.

"I see that you're going to be the next Hawthorne, if you keep this up," he said as he looked at Kimmy. She walked over and snatched her pre-doctoral fellowship certificate out of his hand.

"You don't have to assure me of my well being. I know

my worth. And my mama didn't raise no dummy. I will make it out of these Bricks, and Demetrius is coming with me."

"Let's roll," I said as I made way for Peanut to walk out of the door first.

"I love you so much," Kimmy said as she kissed me one last time.

I waited until I heard her lock the door. Then, I headed to the car. I sat in it, and it was already smoked up with the smell of weed.

"Are you in love with that chicken head? I hope not because you're a G, and you can't be laid all up in some pussy and shit. We have shit to do, like go see these skeezers in the clubs."

"Nah, I'm not in love, but she loves her some black-ass me."

"Go on ahead and light this up," he said as he handed me a blunt. I wanted to ask him about his cousin Ray Ray, but I didn't want to fuck up our night.

I wanted to be in Peanut's shoes one day, but I sure as hell didn't want to be behind bars like Ray Ray. I lit the blunt, and he blasted his radio playing Top Authority's CD. This was the shit that my uncle used to have me listening to ever since I was a little-ass nigga. As I listened to the lyrics and bobbed my head, I sang the hook, saying, "I had to pop 'em. I had to pop 'em. Pop! Pop! Pop! Pop! Pop!"

All I could do was think about the night that I had popped Trevino. I wondered if anyone had found his body yet. Then, thoughts of Kimmy floated in my head. She had said that I couldn't trust Peanut. I was well aware that Ray Ray hadn't been around, but I didn't give too much thought to it. I just thought that, maybe, he was at another trap house or something. And Peanut never mentioned him in any of our conversations. The more I smoked, the more I began to get paranoid.

"Where do you want to go first?" Peanut asked as he handed me another blunt.

"We can go fuck off in Buckhead, or we can fuck off right here on Bankhead."

"I don't care where we go. I just want to have some fun."

I wasn't too fond of calling girls bitches and hoes, but he didn't seem to care. Because every other word out of his mouth was bitch or hoe.

"Let's go to Diamonds of Atlanta. I heard that they got the baddest bitches on the pole," he said as he flew down Bankhead to Rice Street.

When we pulled up, he did the same thing that he always did when we'd pull up at the other clubs. He threw his keys to the valet driver and headed to the front of the line. He never stood in any lines. He slid security a one hundred dollar bill, and, once again, we were in the pussy atmosphere. We walked upstairs, and we sat at the bar and looked down at the dancers who were dancing on the pole below.

This club was all red on the inside, and there were naked girls everywhere. This club was plush from top to bottom. I noticed that there were a lot of people crowded next to me. I got up and slowly walked by, and, to my surprise, it was Gucci Mane. He had an entourage with him. Not to mention, a lot of the baddest girls were dancing for him. The floor was covered with money. And it wasn't just one dollar bills, it was twenties, fifties, and Franklins on the floor.

Peanut came over and got me and said, "You're acting like a stan. I got as much money as that nigga got."

We went to buy two bottles and headed to VIP. He got five thousand dollars in ones and gave me a thousand and told me to throw them. I threw some, and the girls paraded around us. I felt like I was getting the same attention that Gucci Mane was getting. Peanut popped the bottle of rosé champagne, and we sipped and tipped. Peanut looked at me and said, "See. This is what bosses and made niggas do. We wear fly shit, and we come to the club and put on. Plus, we can fuck any bitch we want to. I look at life for what it is. I am a street nigga, and I live by the day, mother fuck another hour. And once I show you the ropes, you'll begin to see what I am talking about."

"What do you mean by 'show me the ropes'?"

"I am saying that it's time for me to make you my right hand man. I have had you under my wing for some time now, and it's time for me to let you get your own bread. You pretty much already know the local fiends around the Bricks. I have to take you to the country with me. That's where the big bucks come in at. They have the work, and all we have to do is collect. This is a dirty game, and everyone in the dope game is all for *self*. Always remember that no one will cover your own ass like you."

The more he talked, the less money I threw. I sat next to him and took in everything that he was saying.

"Does this mean that I will have my own car and trap house?"

"This means that you will have your own everything, your own money, your own hoes, unless, of course, if I want to fuck them, then I will. You will, also, have your own cars. You will have your own Glock. And you will shoot any motherfucker who crowds your space. This street life is nothing to play with. Out here in these streets, it's do or be dead! And I know you don't want to be dead. So, you have to protect *yourself* at all times. And you can't tell your girl your business either. Bitches will use shit against you and get you in more trouble. So, my advice to you is to watch your back and don't trust nobody. And I do be mean nobody. Trust me. I know. I have lost a lot of niggas on that concrete, and it's not a good feeling."

Chapter 17: *The Two Stupid Dogs*

We called it a night and left Diamonds of Atlanta. I thought hard about what Peanut had said about me becoming a made nigga. I wasn't quite sure if I was ready for that, but I knew that I had to help my granny some kind of way. He dropped me back off at Kimmy's apartment, and she was waiting up for me.

"I couldn't sleep," she said as she opened the door. "Every time I saw car lights, I would look out of the window, thinking that it would be you pulling up."

"How long have you been doing that? It's almost four in the morning."

"I thought something bad had happened to you."

"If you think negative, then negative will happen. Think positive," I said as I headed to her bed.

"You smell like weed and baby oil," she said as she unlaced my tennis shoes.

"That's how strippers smell," I said as I buried my head under the pillows. I was drunk as hell, and sleep was calling my name.

The next morning, Kimmy fixed me breakfast in bed. She was my ideal girlfriend. She made sure I was well fed. She fucked the shit out of me, whether I wanted to fuck or not. And she made sure she showed me how much she loved me by telling me every day all day.

"I really don't have an appetite," I said as I held my head, while going to the bathroom.

"Baby, if you eat these sausage links, hot buttered grits, and scrambled eggs, I promise you'll feel a lot better."

I took her word and began to eat. I was only eating because I didn't want to hear her mouth, but I ended up eating all of it because it was so damn good.

"Here. Drink this," she said as she handed me a cold cup of orange juice.

"Come and give me some sugar," I said as I winked my eye at her. "You know that I will never cheat on you, right?"

"I guess I believe you," she said as she put the plate on her dresser.

"Look at me. I am serious. I get pussy thrown at me all day, but you're the only one for me. And I mean that from the bottom of my heart. I want us to grow old together."

"I was thinking that exact same thing last night," she said as she handed me a toothbrush with toothpaste already on it.

"What are you trying to say? That my breath stinks?"

"Hell, yeah! Now, go brush and gargle. You smell like weed, liquor, and girls."

While I was brushing my teeth, I thought about what Peanut had said last night. He said that we were going to take a trip to the country. What if we got pulled over, and he blamed his drugs on me? He did say for me to cover my own ass.

Kimmy came back in the bathroom and hugged me from behind, interrupting my train of thought.

"I will be back. I have to go home."

"You promise you'll be back?" she said as she slapped a fat one on my lips.

"Yes, I promise."

When I opened the door, the sun was shining so bright. It had been a while since I had been home. I didn't really want to go around there because I really enjoyed being at Kimmy's place. As soon as I walked in the door, I saw Uncle Red on the sofa, drunk as usual. And I went in Granny's room and saw Priscilla in there with the insurance man.

"What's going on?" I asked as I walked in.

Priscilla had a surprised look on her face.

"I will tell you as soon as he leaves," she said as she tried to close the door.

"No! Tell me now."

"You should tell him," the insurance man interjected.

"Tell me what? And why are there casket pamphlets all over the bed? My granny isn't even dead yet. Are you planning her funeral already?"

"Yes, I am," Priscilla said as she handed me Granny's life insurance policy. "She has me listed as the beneficiary, and it will only take seven thousand dollars to bury her, so that means I will have over forty-three thousands dollar left after I bury Mama."

"What the fuck?" I said as I knocked the pamphlets out her hand. "You are crazy as hell. You really need to stop smoking crack. There is a fifty-fifty chance that she will live. She's now breathing fifty percent on her own. That means that there is still life in my granny's body."

"I am going to pull the plug, so she won't have to suffer anymore."

"But she's not suffering. She's only resting. How can you even think about pulling the plug on your own mother?

You really need psychological help. The doctor told me that she's doing so much better than before," I said, trying to put some sense in Priscilla's head.

"But, son, we can't afford to keep her on that damn breathing machine. So this is all about money, huh? You want to pull the plug on my granny, so you can smoke all the crack in the world."

By that time, Uncle Red had gotten up and had decided to join in on our conversation. I was waiting for him to say one thing that I didn't like, so I could go upside his head. I wanted to hit Priscilla, but the Bible says honor thy mother. But she had come really close to me punching the few teeth that she had left out of her mouth. I was feeling like I was in the Twilight Zone. This all seemed surreal. She was trying to kill my granny before God called her home.

Uncle Red walked in and sat in Granny's recliner and said, "We all need to just split the damn money three ways, and everybody will be happy."

That was it. I couldn't take it anymore. My blood was boiling, and I had to punch somebody. And his face suited my fists very well. Priscilla was trying to pull me off of him, but I was in a rage. I saw the insurance man out of the corner of my eye as he gathered his briefcase and left. I was pounding on Uncle Red's face, and no one could stop me. I was punching the concrete floor, and my hands were feeling like the bones in them were breaking.

"Get off of my brother," I heard Priscilla say, and the crazy thing was I was her damn son. She was hitting me in my back, but that didn't stop me. My hands were bloody, and I stopped once I heard Peanut's voice.

"Come on, Black Boy. What are you doing? Don't kill the nigga."

I got up and straightened my clothes out and ran out

the door. It never failed in the Bricks. Every time some commotion went down, the whole neighborhood was outside. Peanut's car was parked outside.

He said, "Get in. Let's go before they call twelve on you. Man, I came to check on you, and you in there beating your uncle's ass. What the hell is going on?"

"Man, they trying to kill my granny, and she ain't even dead yet!"

Kimmy came up to the car and asked me, "What's going on?"

"I am going back to the hospital to see my granny."

"Can I come?" she asked as she looked at my bloody hands. "Can you sit in the back seat with me?" she said as she got in the car.

"Hold up. Wait a minute. Do I look like a chauffeur to you?" Peanut jokingly said.

I got out the front seat and sat in the back seat with Kimmy.

"And don't come back," I heard Priscilla shouting as we began to drive away. Uncle Red was on the porch with a towel wrapped around his head.

I thought about what kind of a mother she was and realized that she wasn't one at all. She never did anything for me, not for Christmas or my birthdays. She was a straight up crack head. I really needed for her to be a mother to me. But she loved those glass dicks more than she loved her own mother. So, I knew that she didn't give a damn about me.

"I need to pray for my grandmother, y'all. We all need to pray for her right now, out loud, while we're taking this ride."

Peanut looked at me out of his rearview mirror. I didn't know why he was so surprised. I was raised in the church, and all I knew was God and prayer. Peanut turned Z3's CD down.

"Okay. Let's pray," he said as he lit the blunt that he had in his mouth. I closed my eyes and prayed out loud, "God, please breathe crisp clean air through my granny's lungs. God, please let her open her eyes. God, please bring my granny back to life. God, please thin that blood clot that's in her head. You see what those two stupid dogs are trying to do, and it's not right. God, I beg you to please let my granny pull through this, and I will do everything that she needs me to do. I will take care of her, dear God. Please hear my heart, as well as my mouth, as I pray to you. God, please have mercy on my granny. Amen."

"Amen," Kimmy and Peanut said.

I felt better all of a sudden, but that didn't stop my hands from throbbing. They were swollen, bloody, and hurting. They were hurting so bad that they felt like they had heartbeats.

When we pulled up at Grady, I hit the blunt before I went in. Kimmy was walking behind me with her hand in my back pocket. *This girl must really love me. She wants to be under me twenty-four hours a day*, I thought.

Peanut told me to call him once we were ready to leave. He drove off blasting Z3's CD. Z3 was an aspiring rapper. He was from Zone Three, and he did everything, like producing his own music, mixing down his songs, and making his own beats. He was definitely on the rise in the music industry.

As we walked into the hospital, people looked at me like I should have been headed to the emergency room. I had Uncle Red's blood all over my shirt. We got on the elevator and went to the floor where my granny's room was. The nurse stopped me and asked what happened to me.

"I'm fine," I said as I tried not to show pain as I lifted up my hand.

"You look like you're in pain," the nurse said.

"Never mind me. How's my granny doing?"

"I'll let you see for yourself," she said as she led us to

Granny.

When we walked in, my granny was sitting up in the bed, watching her favorite television show, *Wheel of Fortune.* She didn't have any tubes in her nose. I mean, she looked like my granny again.

"You're alive! You're awake," I said as I fell to my knees and cried.

Chapter 18: *God is Good*

"Of course, I am alive," Granny said as she opened her arms wide for me to come and hug her.

"But a few days ago, you were unresponsive," I said as I went for the strongest hug ever.

"I had a severe stroke that only my almighty God could bring me back from. I bet you were praying just like I taught you. And why do you have blood all over you?"

"Granny, I had to beat the hell out of Uncle Red. I mean, the mess out of him...because he and Priscilla were planning your funeral."

"You mean to tell me those fools didn't even wait and see if I was going to pull through or not?"

"No, Granny, and, on top of that, they were saying how we could all split the money three ways. I wanted to knock some sense into Priscilla, but I know that the Bible says honor thy mother. But she came very close. I don't care about my hands right now. How are you feeling? You scared me to death. We got to get you home, so you can take back over your house."

"She has to stay over the weekend for more

observations," the doctor said as he walked in. "I got to say that it is a miracle that you're even talking."

"That's the mighty work of the God that I serve."

"I want to keep you here because your paralysis even went away. I never, in my forty years of practice, have seen anything like this."

He checked her vitals and said that her blood pressure was back to normal.

"You have to change your diet. No more soul food," he said as he wrote on his clipboard.

"I understand, doctor. I know what I have to do. How are you doing?" she said as she looked over at Kimmy.

"I am doing good. I am glad to see that you don't have those tubes all in you."

"Oh, that's nothing to worry about. God was just telling me that I needed to tighten up."

Kimmy hugged her and sat back in the chair. The nurse walked in and asked if she could have a look at my hands. She examined them and saw that I didn't have any broken bones. She cleaned me up and bandaged me up real good.

My granny was looking like she was back, but brand new. I sat on the bed next to Granny and I just looked at her. Her eyes were no longer brown. They had a tad bit of gray in them. And her hair was turning white as snow. I just sat there, and I thought, *One day, I am going to lose this lady. There will be a time when she will no longer have breath in her body.* I hated thinking about the reality of the situation, but she had always told me that every living thing would one day die.

I kissed my granny on the cheeks and told her that I was going to stay at Kimmy's tonight. She told me not to get in any trouble and to come back and visit her. I called Peanut, and he picked us up.

"So, what's up? Are you hanging with me tonight or

what?" Peanut said as we got in the car. "Or do you have to check in and ask your girl?" He looked at Kimmy and gave her a smirk.

"I don't know what I'm going to do tonight. There is so much going on in my head."

"That's why you need to get out and have some fun."

Kimmy just sat quiet, and I knew what she was thinking. She was thinking that every time he asked me to go somewhere I never said no. I didn't want to have to make a decision like that. I wanted to hang with my boy, but, then again, I wanted to be with my girl. Peanut lit a blunt and handed it to me, and Kimmy covered her nose. He turned the radio up because we were listening to Spice 1's CD. We listened to *Trigga Gots No Heart,* and, once again, every time he played a gangster song, I thought about the night that I had shot Trevino. I wondered if his body had decomposed yet. He dropped us off and said that he would be back to pick me up later. I went inside with Kimmy.

"I know you're not hanging with him again tonight," she said as she slammed the door.

"Look. Don't handle me like I am some pussy-ass nigga."

"Look, Demetrius. Why are you talking like that? You never talked like that before. You are changing, and, if you keep hanging with him, you might be the next one dead or in jail."

"Can you please get off of my case? I am your nigga. You're the only bitch that I'm fucking!"

"Hold up! Wait a minute! You better rephrase that. I am not a bitch. And it's not about who you're fucking. I care for you, and you have so much potential. We are five months away from graduating, and I don't want you to get in any trouble. You can go one night without hanging in the clubs, can't you? Please?" she said as she grabbed my hand, and we walked to her bedroom.

"It's not about hanging in the club. He's going to help me get some money in my pockets. He, also, said that he's going to help me get a car, too."

"Demetrius, you already know that he is up to no good."

"Well, so far everything has been all good. I haven't gotten into any trouble, thus far. And quit speaking negative, my granny told me that the power lies in the tongue. If you speak negative, then negativity will come to you. I don't want to get in any trouble either. All I want to do is help my granny. She's stressing, and, if she has another stroke, she might not be as lucky."

"You're right about that, but, after school, you can go to college."

"There you go with that college shit again."

"All I'm saying is you can go to college and make something of yourself."

I let her continue to talk because there was no winning an argument with her. She always had to have the last word.

Chapter 19: *Da Office*

I continued to listen to Kimmy run her mouth. She had no idea that, when Peanut came back to get me, I was leaving. She was starting to become whiny, and she nagged me a lot. I knew that I was putting the dick down good, but—Damn!— she needed to let a nigga breathe some.

As she talked on and on about *her* future, going to Georgia State University, I tuned her out because my mind was already made up. I was going to be a street nigga. There were no ifs, ands, or buts about it. I had yet to feel what it was like to go to the club and ball with my own drug money. I was ready to feel the draft of the streets. I was so ready for the street life that I could taste it. Then, I thought about how my granny would react once she found out that I was slanging blow. She would have a heart attack, for real. I couldn't put my granny through that, That was why my plan was to work out of Peanut's trap house. It would all work out, if things went according to my plan. There would be no stopping me once Peanut put me down on his team. He said that he was going to show me the ropes. I wasn't a genius in the dope game, but I knew what a dime bag looked like. I heard a knock at the door, and Peanut couldn't have come at a better time. Kimmy just rolled her eyes at me.

I said, "Can I, at least, get a hug because I see that you are mad."

She hugged me and kissed me on my neck. I opened up the door and saw that Peanut was dressed fresh from head to toe. I hopped in the car, and we went to his trap house, so I could shower and change clothes. I took those bandages off my hands and decided that I would just have to deal with the pain. I didn't want to be in the club bandaged all up and shit. I walked upstairs and showered in that scolding-ass water that the Bricks had to offer. One thing about my hood, a nigga would walk around clean, if nothing else. But half of them were too busy to wash their own asses. I let the hot water run on my hands, and, even though there was some pain, it felt good.

"Knock! Knock," a voice said at the door.

"Someone is in here," I replied.

Then, I heard the door open. It was Strawberry, Bankhead's neighborhood whore.

"Girl, didn't I tell you one time that I already have a girlfriend."

"I don't give a fuck. I want to fuck your black sexy ass."

"If I did cheat on my girl, it wouldn't be with junkie bitches. Now, get the fuck out of here before I kick your ass."

"Well, fuck you, too," she said as she slammed the door and left.

I lathered my body up with Coast soap. It was the eye opener for real because it left my body squeaky clean. I hopped out the shower and headed to the back bedroom. My clothes and shoes were still organized. I put on a pair of my True Religion Jeans and a True Religion t-shirt with a pair of 95 Air Max.

Peanut walked in and said, "What did that crazy bitch

Strawberry say to you?"

"Man, I don't know what's up with her."

"I thought that she was lying when she said that she was going to invade your privacy." "Well, she wasn't playing, and she came in the bathroom saying that she wanted to fuck me."

"Well, are you going to?"

"Hell, no! What do I look like? I do have some morals about myself."

"Not me. If there's a hole, I'm fucking," Peanut said as he left out.

"That nigga will fuck anything," I mumbled as I laced up my shoes.

After spraying some Hugo Boss cologne, I was good to go. We got in the car, and Peanut passed me the weed to roll this time.

"I don't know how to roll," I said as I smelled the weed.

"I already cut the blunt. Now, all you have to do is crumbled that weed up and pack it in that blunt. Then, you have to roll it tight. Lick it. Then, dry it with a lighter."

"Damn! That sounds like a lot," I said as I tore the bag open.

The weed was so loud that it smelled like we had a pound in the car. I did what he said, and I lit the end of the blunt. Just as I was about to light the blunt, he said, "Toss it to me and let me see it."

Then, he carefully examined it, like he was looking for any holes or loose spots. He licked the end again, tightened it up, and said, "Now, you can dry it once more. Then, light it."

I lit the end of the blunt and puffed it light because that weed was so damn strong. He turned up the radio, and we rode out of the Bricks with the volume blasting. We rode down to a club called Da Office.

"This spot is owned by a couple named Jack Tre and Jamilah, but I like to joke and call them Jack and Jill," Peanut said as he parked the car. "And his girl is fine as fuck, too, but I don't do my niggas' bitches."

We walked in, and Peanut went to the bathroom. I looked around and observed how decked out the club was. The walls were painted orange, and I noticed that the pool tables were even orange. *This is some fly shit,* I thought as I looked around and noticed signs on the walls that read *Westside Wednesdays* hosted by Mook B and Poka Jones.

I knew a stripper pole from anywhere. I had spotted that when I first walked in.

"So, this is how they do it on the west side, huh? I live right down the damn street and never even thought about a damn club."

I looked around, and I noticed that there were VIP rooms throughout. And the aroma from the kitchen was making me hungry. It smelled like my granny was throwing down back there. And I was amazed at all the big flat screen TVs that were on the walls. They, also, had a poker table room.

Chapter 20: *The Flame*

We stayed and watched Mook B and Poka Jones rock the stage for a few moments more. They both had dreadlocks and looked like they could be kin to Bob Marley. We finished our hot wings and our drinks and left. I had a buzz, but that was all we did when we hung out together. We would smoke weed, drink liquor, and watch plenty of ass. Peanut would call it sipping and tipping at the same damn time. I called it having a damn good time. Because all I knew was walking to the corner church with Granny and watching *Wheel of Fortune*. When we walked to the car, the parking lot was full of cars. They definitely had a full house. They even had strippers, but Peanut said that he only spent his pussy money once, and that would be at the Blue Flame. Peanut said that he forgot to go to Uptown Comedy Corner and check out Scobubble. He was a comedian/pimp from Chi-town, and he had people saying *unnastan me*. We sat in the parking lot for a while and listened to Z3hree's CD. "This little young nigga can rap his ass off,' Peanut said as he turned the volume up. Then, he turned the music down and asked me, "Did you fuck Strawberry?"

"Hell, no!" I almost choked on the blunt. "I wouldn't fuck her with Magic Johnson's dick."

"I am glad you didn't because that pussy is burning like a perm. I can't see how these bitches are so pretty, but they let the streets take over their whole life. I mean, damn! Where is the respect? For example, you got that thick little fine red thang on lock, and she's not sniffing powder or doing the dumb shit that those other bitches are doing in the Bricks. I once had a bitch like that, but I fucked her mama and her grandma. I just didn't give a fuck. This dick don't discriminate. I remember it like it was yesterday.

She lived in Cobb County by the Big Chicken and shit. And she was attending DeVry in Decatur. I was at her house just chilling, rolling up, as usual. And her mama came in the room and asked to hit the blunt, and, the next thing I know, her grandma asked to hit the blunt. Now, keep in mind that her grandma wasn't old like your granny. These were young bitches. The next thing I knew all of that smoking led to both of them choking on my dick. And me being the nigga that I am, I don't turn down jaws or cheeks. So my girl came home, and she shot at my ass. She hit me right here in the back of my leg as I got the fuck out of dodge."

He pulled up the leg of his jeans and showed me the bullet wound.

"She was a crazy bitch, and she's locked up now because, every time she would see me in the streets, she would shoot at me. You see how we're sitting right here chilling? She would do a drive by like she was from Compton and shit. As a matter of fact, I think the bitch was from Compton. I don't give a fuck, though, as long as that bitch is behind bars. I am trying to remember the bitch's name, but, for the life of me, I can't remember it."

I was glad that he had changed the subject and had

stopped talking about Kimmy.

I didn't want to talk about my girl with him. He didn't care about women — period. Not even his own mama. And Granny had always told me that these people in the Bricks weren't my friends. My granny had always told me that a person who didn't respect his own mother didn't give a damn about life period.

"Let's go to the Flame and see some of them red bitches," he said as he backed out. "As soon as I walked in the door, them bitches get my dick rock hard," Peanut said. "And you're a young nigga, so I know that you be about to nut all on yourself."

He was right, but I had a trick to that. I would just sit down until my dick went down. I had done it plenty of times before, but, sometimes, I couldn't help it. Those girls would grind in my lap so hard that I wanted to take my dick out and squirt all over their fine asses. Especially Lolli Pop. She was a thick, tall stallion.

My dick did get hard, just imaging how her ass bounced up and down, but my heart was with Kimmy, and there was no cheating on her. She was a good girl, and I'd have to be crazy to mess that up.

We pulled up at the Flame and Zay the AK was standing in the front like he was ready to go to war.

"What's up with you?" he said as Peanut pulled in.

"Damn! I didn't even know that was you since you cut your dreads off," Peanut said.

"Yeah, man. This is me. I got tired of the dreads."

I noticed that the gun that Zay the AK had strapped on his chest had several extended banana clips. He showed us where to park. We got out and walked in. He stopped Kelley as she flew past us with a clipboard in her hand.

Peanut said, "Bring your slim, sexy ass here. We need a

bottle over here," Peanut said as he gave her three crisp one hundred dollar bills. Then, he stopped Cee Cee and said, "Are you still doing make up for these strippers and keeping these amateurs in check."

She said, "You know it," and walked away.

The VIP area was full, so we stood in front of the stage and watched the amateur night contest. MC Lightfoot was hosting it. He was a fool with it, too. Some of those girls were tore up from the floor up. And he let it be known, too. He told one girl that she walked on stage looking like Whitney Houston, then, when she took her wig off, she looked like Grace Jones. The whole club went wild. Everyone was cracking up, laughing. Then, he told the next amateur, who went up, that she needed to dance like her gas was off. When she kept dancing in slow motion, he said, "DJ, cut the motherfucking music. This bitch is dancing like somebody made her do this shit. Girl, shake that pussy."

The DJ cranked the music back up. Then, the next girl to go up was a big, fat girl. He said, "Hold up, DJ Hershey! Stop the motherfucking music! I will DDT this big bitch right here for three hundred dollars."

A black dude with a mouthful of gold teeth gave him fifteen twenties, and he took off his collar shirt, leaving nothing on but a tank top. He grabbed her and put her in the air, and he did a John Cena wrestling move for real. She got up, walking away like she was used to that shit. The contest was almost over, and MC Lightfoot asked all of the amateurs if they could take an ass slap. Some of them looked like they were professional dancers already. They had asses that looked like amazons, and some of them looked like they needed some of my granny's cooking. One girl bent over, and the dude, who walked up to give her an ass slap, positioned her. She was small and very petite. But that didn't stop him from slapping lightning from her ass. She hurried up off of the stage, holding her ass. I could see the purple bruise that was forming on her behind. The next girl to go up was the big girl from before.

MC Lightfoot said, "Bitch, I bet you can take ten ass slaps."

And once again the crowd went wild again, but no one wanted to slap her on the ass.

Chapter 21: *Meeting of Peanut's Mind*

When it was all over, we had got our money's worth. MC Lightfoot continued to crack jokes and make us laugh. Time was winding down, but Peanut wasn't ready to go home. It was after three in the morning. We sat in the car and waited for a few minutes before pulling off. He put his pistol in his lap and looked around, at our surroundings.

"You can never be too careful. It don't matter that I was born and raised in the Bricks. It doesn't matter that I'm a Grady Baby. These niggas will steal the drawers off your ass and kill you for five dollars. Trust me. I know. I have lost too many niggas to this street life. I have witnessed niggas dying from Hollywood Court all the way to Perry Homes. When you jump in this dope game, you gotta be ready to die for this shit. You gotta be ready to go to war with any nigga. It doesn't matter. Sometimes, you have to go to war with family."

It was a chrome .45. There was a light tap on the window, and he said, "Girl, don't be sneaking up on me like that."

It was Antoinette with her books.

"You see this steel in my lap? I could have easily shot your ass. What do you want? And how many times are you going to try and sell me those same four damn books? Girl, I already got all of your books."

"Duh. I know that. I am coming over here because you are listening to my son's CD. I heard you bumping it when you first pulled up."

"Are you for real? That little nigga Z3hree is your son?"

"Yes, he is my son. His real name is Clyde, and I had him on my birthday. He was eleven pounds even, and I always tell everyone that his head now was the same size when he came out. Because he almost busted my ass wide open. See."

She showed Peanut her tattoo on her arm.

"Well, that little nigga needs a deal because he can rap better than some of this shit that I hear on the radio."

"He will very soon, so just listen out for him. He will be the next superstar."

She started her car with her automatic remote start and left.

"Now, back to what I was saying before that hustling-ass bitch disturbed me. Oh, yeah! When you're in this street life, sometimes, family has to get it, too. There just ain't no way around that. See. Some shit happened to me, and I had to let that nigga Ray Ray take his bid all by himself. See, this is what happened. I was just riding along with him, and it was his drop. We got pulled over with half a brick in the car. And when we do business, we have to own up to our own blow. It's true. He's my cousin, but we was moving his blow not mine. I was just riding, and he got popped. He acted like a man and owned up to his shit. So, he has to do twelve years behind that shit. I have always told him that speeding will get your ass caught every time. He liked to listen to Rocko and shit, too. But, now,

Rocko is out on the town, riding free as a bird in his white Phantom, while his ass is in a four man prison cell. I like to listen to all this hood music, but my uncle taught me to be humble and patient. And that nigga Ray Ray had no reason to speed because it was raining. That is the perfect time to move blow. I might look like a fool and act like a fool at times, but, believe me, I am not a dummy. Why do you think that I haven't been pinched yet? Hold up! Don't answer that. I will answer it for you...because I'm not a fool! Let's ride to Buckhead and fuck around with them white girls."

He put the car in reverse, and we headed on the interstate. I really didn't have nothing to say. I mean, he was always screaming that G shit, and his cousin was doing twelve years. *What kind of shit is that?* I wondered. I had always heard around the Bricks that blood was thicker than water. But, apparently, it wasn't with Peanut.

We rode for a good fifteen minutes, and I read the exit we were getting off at. We got off at Lenox Mall exit. He said that we could just ride up and down this strip. It was Peachtree Road.

"I have blown enough money for the night." He said, "Look at those crackers, jogging at four in the morning. Those crackers are some running motherfuckers until they ass get hit by a truck and die. Or get murdered for life insurance money. Those crackers are the real devils. They are some evil motherfuckers. I watch the ID channel, and they are always doing some off the wall shit. But, then again, our dumb black asses are doing the same shit, too. Just the other day, I saw on the news in New York, a twenty-three year old nigga killed his mama and cut her body up."

"What?" I said as I rolled the window down. I needed some air. The thick, loud pack that we were smoking on made me feel like I was suffocating.

"You heard me right. Black people are doing some horrific crimes, just like these crackers. There was a time when you heard the news, and we already knew that they were white. But, now, when I hear the news and I see that it's us, I be like, 'Damn! What the fuck is the world coming to?'"

"My granny has always told me that we are living in our last days."

"Fuck that. Let me cut you off right there. People been screaming that same shit since I was coming up. I believe that our last days will be when we die. The Bible says that no man will know the hour or the day when God comes. So I don't listen to these damn hypocrites. I'm not calling your granny a hypocrite or nothing. I'm just speaking hypothetically. See, I said a big word that I bet you didn't even know that I knew. Listen to me as I say it again *hypothetically*. Let me take our asses back to the Bricks before I get a damn DUI."

Chapter 22: *Kimmy's Feelings*

When Peanut dropped me off, the birds were chirping. The jays were still walking around like zombies. Kimmy had given me her door key, so I opened up the door and found her in her room, on the computer.

"I'm back," I said as I laid back on her bed.

She must have been into something heavy on the computer because, any other time, she would have run into my arms.

"I see that you're back," she said as she looked at the computer like she had been deprived of sleep. "You told me to find something to do with my time. You told me that I was crowding your space, so I decided to follow that street author Antoinette Smith. She's hot on the social network, and I want you to take me to get my hair done by her stylist Ty. Her stylist is located in East Atlanta, and the name of the salon is ExoTycka. And she can do the hell out of some sew-ins. And I know how you like to see big butts, so you might as well come and see her now. So, when you take me to her salon and see her in person, you won't be shocked and shit."

"Girl, I see big asses all the time."

I took off of my clothes and got under her covers and closed my eyes.

The next morning, when I woke up, she was still sitting in front of the computer.

"Have you been up on that computer all night?" I asked as I cleared my eyes, getting a good focus on her.

"Yes, I have. I am following that street author, and I am looking at her hit up all these clubs, selling her books. Come over here and see her. She's at Blue Flame, and it says that she's at Sheria's birthday party with Shay, Ty, Adamsville Angie, Shameka, and Ne Ne, and they were balling, too. Look at all those bottles of Peach Ciroc in this picture. Here she is at Magic City with Coach Rasheed and his girl Lashunte with a fine-ass waitress named Mary. Look. She put it in the captions under the picture at Magic City. She be everywhere. Here she is with the Official Bread Man at the Ritz. He must be a rapper because he looks like one. And here she is at Justin's in Buckhead with that crazy-ass comedian Karlous. And here she is with her friend Tan and Shonda J. at Club Blaze. Look at this picture. She's right here in Club Blaze with Techwood Ced, Thomasville Stink, and his little cousin Jamal. Oh, my God! Look at all of that money that's in Thomasville Stink and Techwood Ced's hands. That has to be, at least, ten bands. You didn't think that I knew anything about bands, huh? So, that's how they do it at the strip club, huh? I don't see how them girls can take off of their clothes for money. Antoinette is all over the map for real. And did you see her car? She drives a Charger with rims, and her website is on both sides. And her first book, *Daddy's Favorite Pop*, is on it, too. She's really inspiring me to, at least, keep a journal. It says right here on her website that even though she was molested and her mother had her by her step-daddy, pain is not good to keep balled up inside. She said, 'It is not good to keep things balled up inside. Let it all out. I did and look where I came from. You can be whoever and whatever you want to be.'"

She went on and on about Antoinette until I finally stood up in the bed and said,
"I know she sells her books at the Flame because she almost got shot by that fool Peanut last night. We see her at damn near every club that we go to. We saw her at Danny Boy and Poo Poo's spot, Da Fox Phase Two. And we saw her at Da Office. And we were at the Ritz that night when she took that picture with the Official Breadman. He actually performed a hot song with a jamming hook called "Bread in the Kitchen". He got a dance to go with it and everything, but I'm not a dancing-ass nigga."

Then, Kimmy said, "She sells her books from Buckhead to Bankhead. I need to write a book. I need to tell my story, like how my mama is never home. She's always at her boyfriend's house. She hasn't even called to check on me, and that is so unusual for her because she's always checking on me. And how my daddy and I weren't on good terms when he died. That's why I didn't attend his funeral. He left my mama, remarried, and took care of his second wife and her kids. He stopped coming to my dance recitals, and he even stopped coming to see me cheer. Can you believe that? And he had once said that I was his little angel and he loved watching me cheer. But I hate to think about my life because it makes me sad. That's why I have to go to college. I have to make something out of myself because I'll be damned if I am categorized with these girls over here. I hate living in these filthy Bricks. It's already bad enough that there are roaches and rats everywhere. And if they're not shooting every night, the police are chasing somebody. And then, if that's not going on, some stupid girls are fighting over these dumb boys out here. I just want a better life for me, for us. I mean, look at your life. It's fucked up, too. Your granny is doing all she can, but look at your mama and uncle. They don't have the sense that God gave to a damn cat. Those two are hell together. I don't see how they can put her through so much. If my granny was still living, I would take care of her. Not add stress to her life."

Chapter 23: *Change is Good*

Kimmy was still talking about how she was following Antoinette, so I was going to let her meet her because she was very intrigued by her hustle.

"Baby, look. Here is Antoinette again at the Mexican Bar with her homeboy Toby. Do you think he is a rapper?"

"What's with you calling everybody a rapper?"

"I said that because his mouth is full of gold teeth."

"Peanut's mouth is full of gold teeth, and he's not a rapper."

"You have a point," she said as she turned the computer off.

"Aren't you sleepy?" I asked as I gathered my things.

"Not really. I took a nap yesterday. And then I woke up and decided to get on social networking. Everybody at school is always talking about how they are following Ludacris, Z3hree, and Future. So I decided to get on there, and now it's become addictive because all I was doing at first was looking at people's pictures. And I didn't send friend requests to those girls at school because they are full of drama."

"I am about to head home for a minute."

"I'm coming, too," she said as she put on some clothes. She put on my hat, and we headed out the door.

When we walked outside, there were a group of girls standing in the street. I heard one of them say, "You're looking good, Black."

I ignored them, but Kimmy didn't. She looked at them and said, "Sorry, bitches. He's already taken."

"You better be with him like white on rice because if I ever get a hold of him you will be out of the picture."

"Bitch, you wish he would fuck with you. You need to stop sniffing that powder and go find your baby daddy. As a matter of fact, you need to stop fucking up your welfare check and buy your baby some clothes. And he needs a damn haircut because he looks like an extra from the sitcom *What's Happening*."

"Bitch, don't be talking about my baby. Bitch, I will come over there and kick your ass."

"You mean you will try to kick my ass. I'm not scared of neither one of y'all jealous ass bitches. See your ass is just a bunch of mouth, all bark and no biting-ass bitches. You don't want none of this, and who the fuck wears sandals in the wintertime? You need to go buy yourself some clothes. You are a broke-down garbage-ass bitch. You got me fucked up, talking about taking my man, you stupid-looking bitch. Run up, bitch. What are you waiting for? I didn't think so because I will flat line your ass out here."

I couldn't believe that Kimmy was so foul-mouthed. She took off my hat and her earrings. After she started to roll her sleeves up, she was ready to kick some ass. She never talked like that, and those girls were all mouth. They wouldn't bust a grape at a fruit fight. Those other girls didn't say anything either. I guess they had never seen this side of Kimmy, and I hadn't either until today. Because she was always quiet and she stayed to herself in the Bricks. *This girl must really love me,* I thought as I walked, holding her hand. *But living in the Bricks will make you tough.*

We walked in my house and found that Priscilla was asleep and Uncle Red was watching TV. His eyes were swollen, and he had a bandage around his head.

"Nephew, I want to apologize to you. I was wrong and out of pocket. I was dead-ass wrong, talking about splitting Mama's insurance money when she's not even dead. I am going to check myself into rehab. I want to be a changed man."

I wasn't expecting that. He had surprised me with that one.

"That's good, Uncle Red. I am glad you've come to your senses. Because that alcohol is eating you up from the inside out."

"I know it is, nephew, but I wouldn't be the man that Mama raised me if I didn't apologize to you. I have been like this ever since my wife left me. She had my son, and I never saw him since the first day that he was born. Nephew, some people handle life and stress differently. And I know that I fuck up sometimes, but can you blame me? Now, your mama is a different story. I tried to get her to go along with me, but she don't want to go. So, I have to worry about myself and get right with God because Mama raised us in the church, and the church is what I need right about now. I shouldn't be getting pissy-ass drunk. I am almost forty-three years old, and I am still living with my mama. I promise you, nephew, that I will be a changed man. Mark my words! I hugged him and told him that I loved him. That's good, Uncle Red," Kimmy said, "and I am so proud of you. You are definitely doing the right thing."

Chapter 24: *Savannah Bound*

Our house wasn't the same without Granny around. The house started to smell like mildewed clothes. There were no more slow cooking collard greens, pinto beans, ox tails, turkey wings, and cornbread. I really missed those flat iron steaks that she used to marinate and slow cook for hours. They were always so tender and juicy. They were so damn good.

"Damn! I miss my granny. I can't wait until she gets out of the hospital," I said.

Kimmy went in the kitchen and cleaned it. She mopped the floor with Clorox, and she even cleaned the refrigerator out. She really was a good girl, and I knew she loved me because she was ready to take on five girls in the street. We locked up the house and headed back to her house. Those girls were still in the street, looking at us, but they didn't say anything. We heard some music, and it was Peanut.

"Let's take a trip, Black Boy. We have to head to Savannah and holla at my nigga Bigg Dogg Fee."

"I want to go," Kimmy said as she grabbed my hand.

"Damn, girl! You love this black-ass nigga, don't you?"

"Is this the trip to the country that you were telling me about."

"No, it's not the country, but we got to do a transaction."

"Kimmy, you really should stay here because anything can happen."

"Well, if anything can happen, I'd rather be with you."

Peanut looked at us and said, "Get your love bird asses in the car. If some shit do jump off, you'll know for sure if she's really down for you, Black."

We stopped at his trap house and got in another car. It was a four door Honda Accord.

"We will take this low key car right here. It belongs to one of my bitches. My white bitch in Alpharetta to be exact."

We both headed for the back seat.

Peanut said, "Not this time. She has to sit in the front, so, if twelve pulls us over, we can be on some couple shit." She sat in the front and put on her seat belt.

"Who are they?" I said as I noticed a van that read PEEPING TOMS VIDEO SECURITY SOLUTIONZ.

"Oh! That's my boy Rico and his cousin James. They're about to put those flat screens on my wall the right way. I knew I shouldn't have let Speedy put them up because, while I was watching TV, the one in the living room fell. And they're about to put security cameras around my building. I should have been called them to hook this shit up. But I had been using Speedy and the other junkies for lookouts."

Peanut passed me some weed and told me to roll up a few blunts. "This is a four hour drive, so we need to smoke and choke."

He hopped on the interstate and turned on the radio.

"I don't know why that white bitch be listening to cracker music. Every time I get in her car, I throw those country CDs out the window. She be mad, too, but, once I lay this dick down, she don't be mad no more. I forgot to grab that Young Jeezy CD out my car. Oh, well, I guess we gotta ride to the damn radio. I didn't forget this, though," he said as he held up a bottle of blunt spray. "This is some good shit right here, and it has saved me plenty of nights. Those bitch-ass coppers would pull me over and not once did they smell weed. I mean, there were times when I was burning it down in my car, and there goes the blue lights. But this strong blunt spray took care all of that. Let me stop talking about them boys in blue before they get behind our ass."

We rode for a good little minute. Then, he got off to get some gas. We stopped at the Chevron gas station. Kimmy used the bathroom, and I looked directly at a cop car that was parked two pumps over. Peanut quickly sprayed that blunt spray. And he was right. There was not a single smell of weed aroma in the air. We gassed up the car and headed to Savannah. I watched the police officer as he followed us out of the gas station. We hadn't even gotten out of the parking lot good when we heard the police sirens.

"Is this motherfucker pulling us over?" Peanut said as he pulled back into the gas station. "I am pulling back into this gas station, in case this cracker wants to try something. I don't trust they asses, and there are plenty of witnesses at this gas station. Hurry up and get the fuck out of your cop car," Peanut said as he reached in the glove compartment for his license and registration.

"Damn! That's a big cracker," Peanut said as we all looked at the huge cop.

He fixed his shades and headed to the driver's side of the car. Peanut rolled the window down and said, "What did I do?"

"I will ask the questions," the officer said.

Kimmy looked straight ahead, and so did I. I didn't

know if we were riding dirty or not.

"It says on your license plates that you love Alpharetta, but you don't look like your name is Hannah. You're a long way from home, boy. Who is Hannah Pitts?"

"She's my girlfriend."

"Why are you in these parts? And who are these juveniles that you have with you?"

"Why don't you ask them?"

"Nigger, didn't I tell you that I ask the god damn questions? What are you doing in my neck of the woods, boy? You're almost three hundred miles from Alpharetta?"

"We are going to Savannah to see my grandma. She's sick."

"Well, if she dies, that will be one less nigger breathing. Hurry up and get the fuck out of my town, boy."

He hocked up a lot of phlegm, spat on the ground, and sat back in his police cruiser.

"I am so glad that you didn't get back stupid with him," Kimmy said.

"I told y'all that I am not a fool. I am riding dirty. Why would I get smart with that cracker? I have been called a nigger before, and my grandma been dead. So, who's feelings is he hurting? Not mine. I do this shit. My uncle has always told me that, when you're riding dirty, you should remain calm at all times."

We pulled off and headed to Savannah. We got off the exit and road up on Waters Avenue to a restaurant called Bon Tons.

"I'm looking for a beige Jaguar. That will be my nigga Fee."

"There it is, right there," I said as I noticed a tall, slim dude, leaning in the driver's seat. I saw that he had gold teeth, too. He got out, and he was wearing a Polo hat so low that I couldn't even see his eyes. Peanut got out of the car, and Fee walked to the trunk with a duffle bag. They made the transaction, and I knew that Kimmy was scared because I was scared as hell, too. But if I wanted to be a street nigga, I had to get used to shit like those racist-ass cops. Before Fee left, he told Peanut that he wanted us to come to a party that his cousin Chubb was having at Frozen Paradise. And Peanut said that he remembered that one of his homeboys named Juwan from Decatur had told him about the last party that Chubb had had. He said that he had rode down there with Antoinette, Dro, and Dro's girl Stacy. Peanut told me that Chubb was throwing big money and that those bitches was breaking their necks trying to get that money.

"If I'm not too busy, I will make that ride back down here and come to Chubb's party."

They gave each other a high five, and Fee hopped in his Jaguar and sped off, and so did we.

"See! That's what I'm talking about. A sweet drug deal with no problems," Peanut said as he threw me some more weed. As I was rolling it, Kimmy didn't say anything else on the ride back. But I bet she was thinking all kinds of shit, and I knew that I was going to hear an earful once we got back to the Bricks.

Chapter 25: *From the East Side to the South Side*

Peanut got on his cell phone and called College Park Coop. He told him to meet him at the BP gas station on Old National and Flat Shoals. Then, he started to reminisce about his niggas from the West Side that he had lost in the game.

"Damn! I miss my niggas Monkey Man, Quint, Corey, Ray Ray, Mark, Tony T, Mario, One Eye Donnie. Damn! It's just too many to name. God bless the motherfucking dead." Peanut walked into the gas station and came back out with a twelve pack of beer. "Here. Each of you grab four beers, and we're going to pour this shit out for my dead niggas."

"I don't even know how to open beer," Kimmy said, looking at Peanut, confused.

"Damn, baby! You got to be more than pretty. If you're going to be down with my boy Black, you gotta know how to get your hands dirty, but keep them clean at the same time."

She didn't say anything. She waited until he opened the beers for her, and he began to say his dead homies names out loud again. He didn't even care about the people who were looking at us like we were crazy. Peanut sipped out of one of the beers. Then, he poured some out.

"I will always remember my niggas that died out here on these mean-ass streets. It was just last year when my nigga O died, and he was a cool-ass nigga. You just never know when it will be your time to go. These niggas are hungry as fuck, and I don't mind taking a nigga's head off of his shoulders. I will shoot a bitch, too, because it's some rowdy 'bout it bitches out here, too. Some of these bitches out here is harder than some of these soft-ass niggas. Look at that bitch Antoinette. She got five kids, and she sells her books like I sell this blow. She keep her pistol on her at all times because she knows what these streets are about. There that nigga Coop go right there. Get in the back," Peanut said as Coop walked to the car.

"Nigga, you pouring out liquor for your dead homies again?" Coop said.

"Yeah, man. You know I gotta keep it all the way one hundred when it comes to my niggas. Coop, this is my nigga Black, and he is a G in the making. He did some gangster shit, so I am taking him under my wing until he get the ropes of this shit."

Coop had a mouthful of gold teeth, and he often smiled a lot. I guess he was just a happy-ass nigga.

"And this is Kimmy, and she's already taken by my boy Black back there," Peanut said. "I have to let you know because you'll take a nigga's bitch in a heartbeat."

Coop looked at him and said, "Nigga, my plate is full. I don't even have no more room for bitches."

Peanut passed him the blunt and said, "Do you remember all those silly bitches we used to run trains on? They'd suck my dick. Then, they'd suck your dick? Those were the good old days."

"Nigga, every time we get together, you always bring that shit up."

Coop looked at him and said, "Yeah, nigga. I remember all that shit now. Give me the shit, so I can get out of this hot-ass gas station. College Park police been riding around this bitch all day since these young niggas are going around carjacking folks. And you know I keep my iron on me," Coop said as he lifted up his shirt.

Coop got out of the car and left.

I watched Kimmy as she covered her face to avoid inhaling the weed smoke.

"You can get in the back with Black now. I don't need you to sit up here with me anymore."

She happily got in the back seat with me.

"I feel like I am driving Mrs. Daisy with y'all two in the back. But it's all good. We'll be back in the Bricks in a few."

Kimmy laid her head on my chest. When we got back to the Bricks, Peanut parked in front of his trap house. He looked at all of the cameras and said, "Those niggas Rico and James did a good job. Come on up here and check out the rest of the security cameras."

When we walked in, the flat screen TVs were stable, and the security system was top notch.

"This is what I'm talking about," Peanut said as he looked at the monitor that showed the streets. The screen was divided into eight sections, and we could see the whole perimeter around his trap house.

"This is some high alert shit that a nigga like me need. I mean, I got all these guns, but now I got visuals on a nigga."

"Well, I am going to walk Kimmy home, and I will be back in a few."

"Hold up a minute! This is for you, and this is for you." He gave me and Kimmy five hundred dollars each. "That's for risking your freedom and taking that ride with me today."

Chapter 26: *Chilling*

Kimmy and I headed to her house.

"So, what gangster shit did you do to earn stripes with Peanut? I knew that you had done something bad for him to buy you all of those expensive clothes."

"I will tell you everything when the time is right."

"You promise?" she said as she unlocked her door.

"Yes, I promise. Now, fix me something to eat. I'm starving like Marvin."

I turned on the TV in the living room.

"Oh, I know what I'm going to do with my five hundred dollars," Kimmy said as she took some chicken out of the freezer.

"What?"

"I'm going to open up a bank account and save it for when I enroll in college after I graduate. And I know what you can do with yours?"

"What?"

"You can get my hair done."

"I can do that," I said as I flipped through the TV channels.

"I am going to get on the computer until the chicken thaws out."

"Man! Fuck that computer! Come over here and give me some of that pussy."

"Okay. I will. Just let me check something real quick."

I laid back on the sofa, and she came right back, but she still was fully clothed.

"I missed you," she said as she unbuttoned my jeans, "and I really missed him."

She nibbled on the head of my dick.

"He missed you, too. Now, suck him slow. I need some slow head."

She sucked my dick slowly. Then, she spit on it and sucked it fast.

"Come on, baby, and jump on this dick."

"I can't. I'm on my period."

"I don't care."

"Well, I do. That's nasty. How does this feel?" she said as she played with my balls. "Baby, you have to settle for this good head because there is a crime scene between my legs." My dick was sloppy wet, and it felt like I was in some pussy. She was jacking it fast and sucking it at the same time, and, before I knew it, I was busting nuts all in her mouth. She cleaned me up and went to go fry some chicken. I was relaxed, and, as I laid on the sofa, I thought about how disrespectful Peanut was. He was always calling girls out their name in front of Kimmy. I wanted to say something to him, but, then again, I didn't want to mess up what we had going on, but, then again, he was a real nigga, and I was, too, so he'd probably respect it if I checked him.

I got on the phone and called Grady. The nurse told me

that Granny's blood pressure had went up and that she had to stay in the hospital until they stabilized it. But she told me not to worry because they were handling it. I was about to start worrying until she told me that they were treating her with the best medicine.

"Girl, it's starting to smell like my granny's cooking in here," I said as I joined Kimmy in the kitchen. She had thrown down, too. She cooked fried chicken, macaroni and cheese, Glory greens, and warmed up some Hawaiian Rolls.

"I don't know how to cook those greens like your granny, but these Glory greens are good, too."

"It don't matter. Just pass me the hot sauce. I am about to murder this plate."

When I said the word *murder,* I thought about Trevino. I really wanted to tell her about what had happened, but I wasn't sure if I should tell her just yet. Peanut had told me over and over not to let my right hand know what my left hand was doing. And I was going to do just that—keep my business to myself. Besides, if she loved me like she said she did, then she would understand when I did finally tell her. Kimmy wondered off to her room to get on her computer.

I laid on the sofa and thought about how my classmates were going to be sweating me when I went back to school because I was fresh from head to toe. No one would have a reason to pick at me now. I had some of the newest shit. And Bobby said that all I had to do was call him for a fresh cut.

Then, I started to think about Uncle Red. I wished Priscilla would have made a dramatic change like him and turned her life around, but she'd been on crack so long that her brain cells weren't working right at all. She was not even a functioning junkie, like other mamas in the hood were. She had let the drugs take over her mind and body. She used to be so pretty. Now, she had craters in her face, and she was missing a few teeth. She looked just like a crack head. And she was my damn mama, and there wasn't shit that I could do about it. I wondered if an intervention would work for her. She would probably curse everybody out, sitting around, huddled in a circle and shit. Trying to tell her to get her life right. I saw shit like that on TV all the time. And some of those people wanted help, and some didn't even want to be bothered. So, maybe, when she hit rock bottom, she'd want to change then.

Chapter 27: *Something's Fishy*

I smoked a loud blunt by myself, and, before I knew it, I was knocked out on the sofa. Then, all of a sudden, I heard loud banging at the back door. And I knew a police knock when I heard one. Kimmy ran to the door as I was about to answer it. She looked out the peep hole and said, "It's my mother's boyfriend. It's just Curtis."

She opened the door. He looked frantic as he paced the kitchen floor, saying, "Kimmy, where's your mother? I haven't saw her since last week. I don't know where she's at."

"Last I heard was that she was with you."

"Kimmy, the last time I saw your mother was about two weeks ago."

"Well, why in the fuck are you just now telling me?"

"Well, for starters, we got into a heated argument, and she left. I mean, when we argue, we usually have make-up sex, but not this time. She was so pissed off that she left her purse and her cell phone."

"Well, when you noticed that she had left those important things, why didn't you go after her?"

"Because I was giving her time to cool off. Are you sure you haven't heard from her?"

"Hell, no! I thought that she was with you! I am starting to get an eerie feeling in my stomach, and I feel like something terrible has happened to my mama! I can't believe that you haven't seen her in two whole weeks! Now, I am starting to put things together, she always calls me and tells me that she loves me. And, so far, that hasn't happened. I have to file a missing person's report. Curtis, have you thought about doing that, at least?"

"I haven't done anything because I was waiting for her to cool off."

Kimmy sat down at the kitchen table, and I handed her the phone, so she could call the police.

"I just came to see if she was here. I can't wait around for the police to get here."

"And why the fuck not? You're the last one who saw her alive!"

"I just can't hang around. They always suspect the boyfriend in a missing person's case."

"Well, you are showing guilt now, and I haven't even dialed 911 yet."

"You can call me at this number if they need to talk to me."

"So you're just going to leave. You're not even going to stay here with me?"

"I don't like the police, and I haven't taken my medicine today."

"What damn medicine? Are you crazy or something? Did you kill my mother? Please tell me where she is? I won't press charges. I just want to have a peaceful heart."

"I didn't do anything. Call me at that number. I gotta go."

"Demetrius, go after him. I feel in my heart that he has done something to my mother. And he's talking about medicine and shit."

"There's nothing I can do. Just call the police and file the report and give them his information."

"And I never liked that New York motherfucker anyway. He never looked me in my eyes when he came over here."

We waited outside on the porch for the police to show up. When Kimmy saw APD pull in, she flagged them down.

"I want to file a missing person's report," Kimmy said before the officer could even get out of the car. The officer shined the flashlight in Kimmy's face and told her to lower her voice.

"Now, who is it that's missing?"

"My mama is missing, and her boyfriend just came over and said that she's been missing for two weeks."

"Is that not normal for your mother?"

"No, it's not normal for her."

"Hey, I tell you what. Let's go inside and finish filing the report."

We walked in, and the aroma of weed was all in the air. The officer looked around and stood at the back door in the kitchen.

"I need you to fill this piece of paper out, front and back. And please be as detailed as possible."

While Kimmy filled the paper out, the officer looked around. I thought, *Here we go with this bullshit. But, if they do search in here, they won't find anything because I smoked the last twenty of kush that I had.*

"Now, I need for you to write on this blank piece of paper all of the men that she's been with."

"Wait a minute. Are you trying to call my mama a hoe or something? Just because we live in these Bricks, don't mean that she smokes crack and is a hoe."

"Young lady, just do what I asked you."

"She only has one boyfriend, and his name is Curtis Notes. Can you look him up on your police scan or something? Because he was acting suspicious and pacing back and forth like he knew something. Please, officer! She's my mama, and all she does is go to work every day. Here. This is a picture of her. Do you see how vibrant, pretty, and full of life she is. Please don't treat this case like she's one of these crack heads walking around here because she's not."

"Okay. Walk out to my car, and let's run this guy's name."

"Thanks for the change of heart."

When we walked outside, the whole neighborhood was out looking at us. The officer repeated Curtis's name as he entered it into his computer.

"Curtis Ronald Notes has four warrants out of Queens, New York. And it looks like he is a very violent man. He has two for simple assault, one for aggravated assault, and one for attempted murder."

"Murder! Oh, my God! He killed my mama!"

"Young lady, let's not jump to any conclusions."

"Well, what do you want me to jump to? You just read me the record of a maniac. This is the number that he left and said, if y'all need him, call him."

The policeman dialed the number on speaker phone, and the number was out of service.

"Let me try that number one more time."

He dialed it again, and it was still the same, out of service.

Kimmy fell to the ground, and I caught her just before she hit the ground. She kept saying, "My mama is dead. I can feel it in my heart!"

"What kind of car did he come over here in? I can put out an APB on the car."

"I didn't see what kind of car that he was in, and, when he did come over, he was always in my mama's car."

The police officer got on his CB and called Curtis's full name over his police radio.

"Okay. Well, let's start with her car. What kind of car does she drive?"

"She drives a 1993 Toyota Tercel, and it's maroon. And I don't even know the license plates."

"Okay. I will run her name and see what the plates are. In the meanwhile, you call that number and give them this case number, so you can go pick up the police report. Also, if you really feel deep down in your heart that something has happened to your mother, you should check the local hospitals to see if they have a Jane Doe at the morgues. And one more thing, the next time you call the police, make sure you don't have marijuana lingering in the air."

Chapter 28: *Kimmy's Pain*

Kimmy walked in the house and broke down crying. She grabbed her mama's picture and held it close to her chest.

"My daddy is dead, and now there's a chance that you are dead, too."

I didn't want to bring up a life insurance policy at a time like this, but this does not look good on any level.

"Baby, did your mama have life insurance?"

"Yes, she has life insurance. But I will check the hospitals first to see if they have any Jane Does."

"Your mama hasn't really known him long enough to let him in her life like she did. I mean, I remember when she said that she had met him walking down Fulton Industrial. That was a big red flag right there," I said as I grabbed her hand.

"He used to creep me out, too, because he would always walk to her room slow, peeping in on me in my room."

"Dang, baby. Those are warning signs that you should have brought to your mama's attention."

"I know, but I didn't think much of it because she was so in love with him. But she hasn't even known him for a full year yet. But I am so in love with you."

"That's because we've live in these Bricks, and we have known each other our whole lives."

"Well, why haven't you ever told me that you love me back? I mean, I tell you all the time. But you never tell me, and I need love more than anyone right about now."

"Girl, I do love you. I just don't express myself like you do. But trust me. I do love you, and I want you to be my wife one day. And you will be the wifey with two e's because you are energetic and everlasting on this dick. But, in all seriousness, I do love you, baby."

"And I want you to be my husband, too. I can see us walking down the aisle now. You will have on a black tuxedo with a red tie. And I will have on a long white dress with a red veil over my eyes."

"So, you want us to have a red and white wedding, huh?"

"I don't care what kind of wedding we have as long as we grow old together. You are my soul mate, and I knew that ever since we used to walk to church together when we were younger."

"And I knew that you were my soul mate when you ate in the dark with me when our lights were cut off. I knew that you were my soul mate when the kids teased me at school about my clothes. You didn't join in with them and neither did you laugh along. I been knew that you were loyal. Come over here and let me dry those tears that are falling down your face. Everything will be alright. Even if something has happened to your mama, we still have each other. We will always have each other, no matter what. Look at me. We are going to be alright. Okay?"

"I believe you. I just can't believe that this is happening to me right now. I know that a parent should go before the child, but she's only forty-three years old. She was just talking about how we were going to go on a vacation to Jamaica. And now this. I may have to bury her. I can't face my mama in a casket. This isn't fair at all. God, why does this have to happen to me? And I don't believe in that 'everything happens for a reason' shit either."

"Hold up, baby! Don't curse God. He didn't do it. But He sees and knows everything."

"So, why did my mama have to die? Baby, we don't know that for sure yet. Come on, baby. Let's pray right now because you are letting your emotions take over now. You remember how we prayed hard for my granny? And now look at her. She made a full recovery from a stroke. Now, you can't tell me that God isn't good, and I will not let you sit up here and curse at God neither. Now let's get on our knees like how we used to do at Sunday School. And stop crying, baby. Everything is going to be alright.

God, we come to you with our souls and minds open to you. Please keep your hands on Kimmy's mama. God, please don't let any harm come to her. I pray to you, God, that there is some magnificent explanation as to why she hasn't been home in two weeks. God, we will not speak negative on her mama's soul. We will speak only positive things from this day on out. So, in Jesus' name, we pray that you will bring her home with not one hair harmed on her head. Amen. Do you feel better now?"

"Yes, I feel a lot better now. Now, all I need for is my mama to walk through that door."

"She will come home. Don't worry. All we have to do is let go and let God."

"Demetrius, letting go and letting God is the hardest thing to do. I know, when I listen to Yolanda Adams and she says, 'Give it to Jesus.', that's easier said than done."

"Baby, that's when you have to jump into faith mode. We have to believe in His word. He will never leave us, nor forsake us. You know how strong the power of prayer is, and I hate to say this, but it's right next to the power of pussy. I just want to put a smile on your face, baby. I know that you are hurting right now. But please believe me when I say that God will see us through this. One day, we're going to look back at this day and laugh. Now, what if that pussy-ass policemen had taken us to jail for the weed smell in here? I mean, we have rights, but they are so dirty and crooked nowadays."

"Who knows? He probably would have planted some weed in here."

"I know that's right, and what about the one from Savannah today? What if he would have searched that car? We would be under the jail. That's just goes to show how good God is. Now, get that deck of cards, and let's play two hand spades."

"I want to play UNO."

"It don't matter. We can play I declare war, and I will still win."

"Oh, yeah! Let's play that one. I haven't played that in a long time."

"And put on that Meek Mills CD. He be going hard."

"Baby, you kind of look like him with those deep waves in the top of your head."

"Yeah, but I think I look better," I said as I rubbed my chin.

Just as she began to deal the cards, there was a knock at the door.

Chapter 29: *Up All Night*

I turned the radio down, and we both went to the door.

"Who is it?" Kimmy asked.

"It's me. Peanut."

She opened the door, and he walked in with a big brown paper bag.

"What's up, y'all?" Peanut said as he put the bag on the kitchen table.

"Hey, Kimmy. Hold your head up. Your mama will turn up soon."

"How do you know about that?"

"Girl, we live in the Bricks, and the streets are talking. Plus, I know everything. And I wanted to hang out with my slick partner tonight, but I know that he has to stay in and be by your side at this difficult time. So, that's why I brought us something to drink and a few goody bags." He reached under his shirt and put his pistol on the table. "This is for you." He threw me some weed. And he said, "And this is for me."

It was some powder cocaine.

Kimmy looked shocked as she said, "Well, I don't do

neither. I don't drink nor do I care to ever try drugs for the first time. Those drugs are not good for you. Do you know what those drugs do to your body?"

"Yes, I know what they do to my body. This cocaine keeps me wide awake and on my Ps and Qs. And this good-ass loud keeps my dick hard all night."

"Wait a minute. Man, can you stop talking like that around her?"

I had to say something because he had no respect for women, but he would show some respect for my girl.

"Damn! My bad, Black Boy. You got my word from now on. I will watch my mouth around your girl. I know that y'all are two love birds. But I'm just a hood-ass nigga, and I just say shit without thinking. But I'm glad that you stepped to me like a man in front of your girl. That's some boss shit. I can't do nothing but respect that. Now, let's get this night started," Peanut said as he took off of his jacket. "I wanted to go fuck off on Old National at the El Ranchero Mexican Bar. I wanted to go in there and buy a few bottles and watch Blu, Bigg, Mean, and Rico throw them fools out on their heads when they get drunk and act a fool in there."

"Oh, I heard about that Mexican bar! I am following that street author Antoinette Smith, and she has so many pictures of her in there, selling her books. She talks about how she always parks her car in VIP everywhere she goes. She said that when she parks at the Mexican Bar, Cedric Williams from California parks and watches her car all night. She's such an inspiration to me."

"If she's that big of an inspiration to you, I can call her over here for you to meet her."

He called Antoinette's cell phone. When she answered, she said that she was in Miami with her man Dee. But she did say that she would meet Kimmy when she came this way to go the Flame next week. I told her that she could meet her anytime because she stayed in the streets, selling them damn books.

Peanut looked at Kimmy and said, "May I have a cup of ice please?"

The look that he gave her wasn't a friendly look either; it was a seductive look. She grabbed a bowl and filled it up with ice and put it in the middle of the table. He opened up the bottle of Hennessy and looked at me and said, "Nigga, grab a cup. I'm not about to drink all of this shit by myself."

"We were just about to listen to the radio and play I declare war. Do you want me to deal you in?" Kimmy said.

"Hell, yeah! I love that game, even though I haven't played it since I was little."

Peanut pulled out two quarters and crushed up his bag of powder. Then, he rolled up a one hundred dollar bill. He stuck it in the baggie and sniffed away.

"That's the good shit right there. This is fish scales, and it's so potent. Just how I like my blow. This shit right here drain quick as hell. I make sure I don't get no rerock or stepped on work. My uncle taught me about blow when I was a little nigga. He used to let me taste the shit when I was around eight years old. And he said, 'See. That numb feeling on your tongue means that it's some good shit.' Then, he took a corner off of a brick and said, 'Always look for the crystals shining in the blow. This is what we call fish scales.' Damn! I really miss my uncle. He's the realest nigga, besides myself, that I know. But he was a good teacher because this is that one hundred percent pure uncut Colombia blow. I crumbled up the weed and rolled a few blunts up. Kimmy stood out like a sore thumb because she was a good girl and she had a leveled head. She knew what she wanted to do with her future, and she wasn't going to let nobody destroy that.

Chapter 30: *Quiet as Kept*

While Peanut was still reminiscing about his uncle, I started thinking about my granny. Then, Kimmy started to worry about her mama again. We all got sad all of a sudden. Kimmy even took a shot of Hennessy. We all were some drunk and high fools. It was daybreak, but Kimmy and I called it a night and went to bed. Peanut said that he wasn't too drunk to drive to the other side of the Bricks. Kimmy laid on my chest, and I heard her crying herself to sleep. But all I could do was hold her.

The next day was Sunday, and we laid in the bed for a little while longer than usual. I was hungover, and she was, too.

"I love you," she said as she turned over to kiss me.

I kissed her and held her close.

"I know you do," I said as I held her tighter. I was going to tell her that I loved her back, but it was going to be when I was ready to say it.

"Are you ready for school?" she said as she got up.

"Hell, yeah! I am ready for school. I am ready to wear my new shit. I am ready to see some faces crack literally. I can't wait until that motherfucker Lenny sees me in my new Jordans and my True Religion."

"I can't wait either, baby. I used to feel so bad for you when he used to clown you in front of the whole class."

"But that's cool because I made his pussy ass eat those words. And he ended up being the clown-ass nigga. Because he always ended up with blue and black eyes with red busted lips."

"Yeah, I gotta admit. You did beat his ass every time he made fun of your clothes. And I enjoyed watching every minute of it."

"I hate bullies, and he was the whole school's bully. Fuck Lenny. Let's catch the bus downtown and go see my granny."

We walked to the bus stop, and all eyes were on us as we walked through the Bricks. When we got to the hospital, Granny was asleep. The nurse walked in and said that she had to stay a little while longer because her blood pressure was too high for her to go home.

"Well, is she going to wake up?"

"She is heavily sedated, and she's been sleeping a lot lately. But everything else is going very well. The blood clot that caused the stroke has thinned out. So when we get this blood pressure under control you can have your granny back."

I kissed Granny, and we left.

Kimmy and I decided to do a little shopping downtown. We went to the Bootery to get her some pink Timberlands. And then we walked across the street to Eddie's. I wanted some pull out gold teeth.

"Are you serious about wearing those things to school?"

"Yes, I am dead-ass serious."

"Well, I won't kiss you with those things in your mouth."

"That's cool. That's why they are called pull outs. Duh. I can pull them out."

"You look sexy with them, though."

"Well, give me some sugar."

She kissed me.

"I thought you said that you wasn't going to kiss me."

"I couldn't resist," she said as I paid for them and left.

When we got back to the Bricks, something was different. It wasn't normally that quiet unless the Red Dogs came through here and did a sweep. I mean, there was not even a junkie out.

"These Bricks are finally quiet," Kimmy said as she unlocked the door.

"Yes, they are, but the police probably came and did a sweep."

"They need to sweep all these junkies into the sewer. I'm sorry. I didn't mean to say that. I know that your mama is on drugs."

"I don't have no hard feelings. I mean, she is a junkie. You're just calling it like you see it. I will be right back I am going to go to Peanut's trap house and bring my clothes over here."

"I'm coming with you. I can't believe that Speedy isn't even out here."

"Me neither," I said as I unlocked the door.

Peanut's trap house smelled just like cooked dope. I looked around and saw that all of the security cameras were still recording.

"Demetrius, maybe, you can rewind it and see if something happened out here today."

I took her advice and pressed the rewind button. And

sure enough, the red dogs had come through there with masks on. They didn't show their faces because they were afraid that the dope boys would get revenge on them. But I didn't see Peanut anywhere in the vicinity. Maybe, he was with one of his freaks that he always talked about. Kimmy helped me with all my bags and shoes. When we finally got back to her house, she made room in her closet for my things. She hung my clothes up and lined my shoes in the closet on top of the shoe boxes. So, now I had some of my clothes at all three apartments — the trap house, Kimmy's house and my house. Then, she looked at me as I put one of Peanut's guns on her night stand.

"Where did you get that from? And do you know how to use one of those things? Demetrius, that's a real gun. That is not a controller to your video game. This is not *Call of Duty*. That's a real gun with real live ammunition."

"Kimmy, I know what this is, and we're all we got. These streets are crazy, and we don't have no one to look after us."

"What about God?"

"I mean God is always there, even when bad things happen. This is just for extra protection. While we are laying in here by ourselves. You know how it gets in these Bricks. They will think that we are vulnerable and fuck with us because your mama is gone and my granny is in the hospital. So, wouldn't you rather that I protect us at all costs, or would you rather be another statistic in these damn Bricks?"

"Well, since you put it that way, show me how to shoot it because one day I just may have to use it."

I called Peanut, but his cell phone went straight to voicemail. Kimmy and I took a hot shower and got ready for school the next day. I knew that Kimmy was depressed because of her mama because she didn't even jump on my hard dick.

Chapter 31: *Back to School*

I woke up before the alarm clock went off. Kimmy was still asleep with a pillow between her legs. She looked so peaceful while sleeping. I had gotten my fresh cut from Bobby the night before, so now I was ready to put the gold teeth pull out in my mouth. I had bought a grill for the top and the bottom. I was so ready to go to school. I knew, for a fact, that I would be the center of attention, but it wouldn't be funny.

"I can't wait to see their faces when I walk in the school. I'm willing to bet that all of the other students will be looking at me from head to toe. I know I will make a couple of folks sea sick with these deep waves in my head. And they're going to really be mad because Bobby hooked my haircut up to perfection. He even lined my goatee up with a sharp razor."

I walked in the kitchen and fixed us some cream of wheat and turkey sausages. That Captain Crunch cereal looked good on top of the refrigerator, but Granny had always told me that I was a growing boy and that I needed solid foods. I heard the alarm clock go off and in walked Kimmy to the kitchen, moping around slowly. I was at the stove, and she came behind me and kissed me on the back of my neck.

"I see that you're up and ready to go to school. Ooh, baby! That looks good. I love grits."

"Thanks for the compliment, but these are not grits. This is cream of wheat."

"Same thing," she said as she went to go put on her clothes.

I sat at the table and began to eat my breakfast. I tried to wait on Kimmy, but she took too long.

"Your food is getting cold!" I hollered as I put my plate in the sink.

She didn't answer me, so I went to find her. And I wasn't surprised when I found her glued to that damn computer.

"So, who is Fifty from College Park?" I said as I snuck up behind her, reading her Facebook page.

"I don't know who he is, but I saw this picture of him and his little girl. Look at her. She's a doll, isn't she?"

"Yes, she is very cute. Now, let's go before we are late for school."

"Okay. Wait a minute. I have to check that I like his other pictures of him and his daughter. And the school is directly across the street. We're never late."

I had no reason not to trust her, but I had heard that those social sites broke up happy homes. But just in case, I would keep my eye on her and Mr. Fifty from College Park.

"One last thing, baby. Look at Antoinette again. Here she is at Da Fox Phase Two with a waitress by the name of Taila. She took a picture with her holding a copy of her book *Married, Sneaky Black Woman.*"

"I remember seeing Taila in there because Peanut said that she was one of the finest waitress in there. And look at her right here in Las Vegas with her friend Trina."

"Oh, baby! Look at that pretty clear blue water. Can we

go to Las Vegas and get married? And here she is posing for the camera with Brandon the professional photographer who is always at all of the clubs all over Atlanta, taking the best pictures. And look at her again right here at Club Déjà Vu with the handicapped hustler Carl C. And who is Blueberry Pimp?"

"Oh, I know who that is," I said as I looked closer. "He's the manager at El Ranchero Mexican Bar. I, also, decided to follow Antoinette's cousin, Erica Redmon, who appeared on the T.I. & Tiny's *Family Hustle*. Okay. Now that's enough."

I turned off of the computer.

"I'm sorry, baby, but I think I am addicted to the computer," she said as she locked the door.

It was January, and it was cold outside. Kimmy had put on a pink sweat shirt with a pair of tan Levis with her pink Timberlands. After she grabbed her food and raked some of it between two pieces of bread, we headed to school. I grabbed the gun and put it under my shirt.

"Why are you bringing that to school with you? The metal detectors will go off when you walk through."

"Come on now. You and I both know that those things don't work. When was the last time they worked? I am carrying this because these niggas be going around, robbing for these shoes that I have on. These are the 95 Air Maxes, and some kids have actually died over these shoes. Over a pair of shoes— period."

"Yeah, you're right," she said as she threw the end pieces of her bread in the street. "I still want you to show me how to shoot it because I don't trust these motherfuckers either. Maybe we can go behind Carter G. Woodson Elementary school and shoot in the woods."

"Kimmy, all you have to do is pull the safety off, pull the trigger, and aim at a motherfucker's head."

As soon as we walked into the school parking lot, I heard

some loud music, and I knew that it was Peanut. He told me that he wanted me to ride with him to Etheridge Court Apartments. Kimmy and I walked in the school, and, just like I predicted, there were several jaw dropping onlookers looking at the both of us. They were looking at her because she looked pretty in her pink. Plus, Ty had hooked her sew-in up. I didn't know much about hair, but I knew that it was some good hair because it had cost me a good grip.

After I walked Kimmy to her homeroom class, I preceded to walk to Mr. James' classroom. He was writing on the board as I walked in. I sat down at my desk, and I saw Lenny out of my peripheral vision. He was dressed nice, but he didn't come close to what I had on. He wore the Tommy Hilfiger, Polo with Eastlands or Polo Boots. But if it came down to a battle in a dressing contest, I would win because my True Religion pants had cost more than his whole outfit, including his shoes. For some reason, I felt like a star. I knew that I had eyes stabbing me in my back, especially since I sat in the front of the class. Ever since I had beat the shit out of Lenny, Mr. James had moved my seat permanently to the front, close to his desk. Lenny sat in the back, and I knew for sure that he was breaking his neck, trying to check out my gear. I must say that I looked like a new nigga.

Mr. James turned around and did a double take when he saw me sitting there, looking like a million bucks. He pretended to teach the class, but I knew that he saw that big-ass platinum chain around my neck. Everyone saw it, even the principal with her crack smoking ass. She must have thought that I was a new student because, as soon as she realized that it was me, she quickly turned her head. I didn't want to see her ass anyway. I wanted these students to see how I had just up and transformed on their asses.

It was time for us to change classes, and, as soon as I

got up to leave, Mr. James asked to have a word with me. And as soon as Lenny walked by, I looked him directly in his eyes with my mouth slightly open, so he could see the glamour shining in my mouth. I thought, *Yeah, now take that, fuck nigga.*

"So, what do we have here?" Mr. James asked as he closed the door. He told the other students to hold up before entering the classroom. "Why are you looking like those fools in the Bricks over there? And what do you have in your mouth? Demetrius, trust me, son, you do not want to take that route. Do you remember when I told you about taking boxing classes?"

"Yes, I remember."

"Well, I have an old college buddy who has his own boxing camp. His name is Breylan, and the name of his boxing camp is called Breylan's Champs Boxing Camp. He's a really good friend of mine, and I have known him for years, and he's always doing something productive for our youth. I think that this would be really good for you. Because, if you hang out with that fool Peanut, you're going to end up like his cousin Ray Ray."

"How do you know about Ray Ray?"

"I know that he'll probably be somebody's bitch behind those bars. He has a twenty year sentence. And how old is he now? Like twenty six? Now, add twenty years to that. He will be almost fifty years old when he gets out. That's if he make it out alive. Demetrius, you have to think about the consequences. And what about Kimmy? Do you want to mess that poor girl's future up? And I know more than you think I know. I know that you almost beat your uncle into a pulp. And I, also, know that he's in rehab. But what I want to know is, how is your grandmother doing?"

"She's straight."

"She's what? So, now you're talking that slang language, too? Well, I am glad to know that she's feeling better. And, son, it's not where you live; it's how you live. And I can tell right now that you're feeling yourself and you don't want to hear anything else that I have to say. Why are you laughing? I *am* familiar with young people's talk. You didn't think I knew what 'feeling yourself' meant?"

"I never heard you say anything like that because you're always speaking that black power positive shit."

"Demetrius, I am simply breaking things down to your level. I was your age once, and the same thing was going on when I was coming up. I told you my life story because I feel that you can make a difference as well. I want you to be a part of the solution, not the problem. I know that you have a dysfunctional family. Hell! Who doesn't? But the question at hand is, what does Demetrius want to do with his life? I'm not going to preach your ears off, but there's going to be a time when you'll wish that you had had somebody like me to talk to. I will never steer you wrong. Now, go on your next class and please consider taking me up on my offer."

I walked out of the class, thinking, *I am already a made nigga because Peanut had told me that I was already a G.*

Chapter 32: *Goose Chase*

Kimmy and I met up in front of the school and headed home. Peanut pulled up and told us to get in. Kimmy said that she would walk.

"Girl, don't act like that," Peanut said. "I don't have any drugs in here."

We both got in, and I walked her to the door. She hugged me tight and told me that she loved me. I told her to lock up and that I would see her later.

"I love you for real," she said loud enough for everyone to hear.

"I know you do. Now, go on inside and lock up."

I got in the car, and Peanut didn't waste any time passing me the blunt.

"Did you have any problems in school today?"

"Nope. Everything went good as hell because everyone saw me looking like money."

"I know that feeling," Peanut said as he turned the music down a tad bit low. "I am supposed to meet with my homeboy Marc in Etheridge. And then we have to meet up with an associate of mine. So, until then, we can go chill at Diamonds of Atlanta. I wish that Treasure, Skittles, Ambitious, Luscious, and Paradise's fine asses was at work at the Blue Flame, but they work the night shift."

"You mean to tell me that you go to the strip club in the daytime, too?"

"Hell, yeah. Why not? Those day shift bitches gotta make money, too. I wish I could go see my girl Stamped Infinity because she's a world-renown stripper."

When we pulled up, there was a crowd of cars in the parking lot. We walked in, and he did what he always did, walk around and speak to people that he knew. Then, he came and got me and told me to come with him to the DJ booth. As I looked around, I noticed that there were pictures that read DJ Cloud with a few celebrities like Young Jock, Tommy in the City, Z3hree, Future, Gucci Mane, Rocko, and Cash Out. Peanut looked at him and told me that he was an old school DJ. He used to deejay at Club Nikki's before it went up in flames. He had been a DJ at damn near all the strip clubs in Atlanta. I remember when he used to deejay at the Blue Flame. Then, he looked at DJ Cloud and said, "Man, why do y'all DJs hype the crowd up to throw money at some of those ugly girls? I know damn well that you have seen what I have seen on the stage, and all of those girls just ain't pretty. I like to see some bad bitches on the pole."

DJ Cloud said, "Man, I love all women, and this is their job, and they have children to feed, car notes to pay, and, most importantly, they have to keep a roof over their heads."

"Well, I guess you do have a point. Besides, ugly hoes need money, too."

Peanut threw a stack of ones in the air, and we left. When we got to the car, Peanut got on the phone and said that his associate had headed to the East Side. He said that he didn't realize how long he was talking to DJ Cloud in Diamonds of Atlanta. It was getting dark, and time had flown by. So, when we got off at Moreland Avenue, he called his associate again, and he told him to go to Club Blaze. When we walked in, there was a banister hanging in VIP that read Happy Birthday, DJ Big C. There were red and white balloons everywhere.

DJ Big C must have been a pretty wealthy man because he had the other VIP section as well. Each one of the VIP booths had so many bottles that they looked like the bar area. As I looked around, I saw that those girls in there was fine like the girls at the Blue Flame and Onyx. Then, Peanut walked up to this tall dude, and it must have been DJ Big C.

Peanut said, "I know that you're not spinning in this motherfucker tonight."

DJ Big C said, "Hell, no! I am celebrating my birthday. I been working in here for nine years, and it feels good to sit back in VIP and ball in this bitch tonight."

He dapped DJ Big C up, and we went to go sit at the bar. He told me that it's a must that I keep my face card good. He told me that, if he was fucked up in the pocket, that he would be able to go to anybody that he knew and bounce back. He even named a few rappers who he said that he could get some money from if he needed it. He ordered us both a shot of vodka, and we sat there and listened to Lil Boosie's "No Mercy". Then, he went on, saying how Lil' Boosie was a real-ass nigga. After a few minutes, he looked at this phone and said, "Damn! What's taking this nigga so long to get here? This nigga hasn't called or texted my phone. Man! Fuck it! Let's ride. Twelve probably got behind him because he's a flashy-ass nigga. I mean, he will speed in front of the police, and he might have a kilo in the trunk."

We headed back to the west side, and his associate called him on the phone and told him to come to Etheridge. Peanut hung up the phone and said, "That nigga must think that I am a duck or something. It's bad enough he got me riding around like a chicken with my head cut off. And I am trying to give him some work. I hate working with new niggas. But I have been in this game long enough to know bullshit when I smell it. And for this nigga to have me riding from the west side to the east side and then back to the west side, he sounds like he might be working with them folks. Let me throw this phone away. That nigga might be working with the police."

"You just threw your phone out of the window," I said, astonished.

"Hell, yeah! I had a vibe about that nigga anyway the first time I dealt with him. My cousin Ray Ray turned me on to him. And when I first met with that country-ass nigga, he didn't even know a damn ounce from a gram. Sometimes, you have to turn some money down because all money ain't good money. It's called greed. At the end of the day, greed will get you fucked up. So, now let me tell you what the move is for you. I want you to go take over my trap house. I think that it's time that I settle down with one of my bitches. I'm just playing. I will be a player for life. Fuck these money hungry hoes. But, for real, I want you to hold it down. I will show you how to cook, weigh, and bag up the dope."

"You actually want me to go live up there after the red dogs came through and swept that motherfucker clean?"

"The red dogs came, but they didn't fuck with the trap house. They got those nickel and dime young niggas and those stupid-ass junkies. They even got Strawberry's ass, and they got Speedy. And you know that Speedy was a functional junkie that I had running it, but he violated parole, so he will be gone for a minute. It's sweet as pie. That's why I had all of those cameras installed. I even know about the gun that you took."

"How did you know about that? I mean, I wasn't

stealing it or anything. I just wanted to have it around for protection."

"I understand. And you're going to need more than that pistol once you become the man out here in these streets. But Rico from Peeping Toms downloaded an application on my phone, and that is how I saw you when you took the gun. See. Look. I will show you."

"Wow! That's tight," I said as I looked at his phone and saw his whole trap house.

Chapter 33: *Running the Trap House*

Peanut and I went into the trap house, and he did exactly what he said that he would do. He cut open a brown block and carefully peeled all the sides back. He threw the plastic in the trash and put the brick of cocaine on the kitchen counter.

"See. You smell how strong that shit is? I want to take a one on one right now because this shit is so potent. Fuck it! Don't mind if I do."

He sniffed more like a three on three in each nostril.

"This right here is what we call a block of cocaine. And this red stamp on top makes it official. I get my work from a Columbian, and, if Pablo Escobar was still living, I would be getting my blow from him. Look under that sink and give me that Vision Ware Pyrex pot. The medium sized one will be good. Now, when you're cooking blow, you have to know your measurements. You have to use the right amount of water. If you use too much, you'll fuck it up, and you will be in this kitchen all day, trying to bring that motherfucker back. Some niggas use baking soda to try to stretch their blow, but those are those broke ass niggas who don't have a connect like me. If you want to have all the junkies to yourself, don't ever step on your blow. So, watch me very carefully as I make this powder turn to hard crack cocaine.

I will bag half up for the powder heads, and I will cook the other half for the dope fiends. And make sure that you weigh it up on the scale in the bag. You see how I just did that with it in the bag? Now, look at how the number changes when I weigh it without the bag. And you gotta watch these junkies, too, because they will try to play you and get extra blow."

"Hold up! Wait a minute! I just thought about something. Are you going to be watching me and Kimmy have sex with all these cameras around here?"

"Nigga, are you serious? Are you asking me about some pussy when I am showing you how to put some money in your pocket? Please don't let pussy be your downfall. Do you know how many Kimmys you're going to have? Now, focus on this dope class that I am teaching you. So, listen to me and watch me very carefully because I am showing you how to make yourself a boss. This is the same shit that my uncle did to me. Rest in Peace, Unk."

He mixed that dope like he was a chemist. When he cooked up an ounce of dope, he made me go right behind him and cook up an ounce of dope. He showed me how to weigh the dope with and without the scale.

"So, when do you want me to start?"

"It looks like you're on the clock now because the fiends are marching through the hood."

"I need to, at least, let Kimmy know that I will be over here for a while."

"There you go again, thinking about pussy when you have about two thousand dollars coming up the steps. Look!

Keep it real with me right now. Do you want to do this shit? Or do you want to go back to living like an episode of *Good Times*?"

"Fuck, no! I am going to get this money."

"That's what I want to hear. And don't be afraid to use one of those choppers on somebody if push comes to shove. You know that robbing comes with this shit, too. So you have to have a pistol on you at all times. It's best to get caught with a pistol than to get caught slipping without one. Now, with that being said, you have to get familiar with the faces of your customers. Yes, I did say customers. You have to treat this shit like a career. You have something that half of the world is on. And I don't care what nobody says, it can be zero degrees outside, if you have work, then you will always have money in your pockets. Now, I am about to get out of here. I have some other business to take care of. Call me on my cell phone if you need me. Remember what I said, money over everything."

When he left, the junkies were lined up at the front door. Some were scratching themselves, and some just looked like they were three breaths away from death. I was praying that I didn't see Priscilla in that line because, if I did, this shit would have been over. I couldn't believe all of the fives, tens, and twenties that I had accumulated in a matter of minutes. The money was coming so fast that it made my head spin.

When the trap house traffic died down, I walked to Kimmy's house. I walked in, and she was on that damn computer again.

"Who are you following now?" I asked as I laid back on the bed.

"I am following somebody named Lil' Forty, and, from what I see, he's all over Atlanta. Here he is at Club Solutions with an entourage. Oh, my God! And here he is with that street author Antoinette. I really want to meet her."

"Okay! That's enough talking about other niggas."

"Awww! Is my baby getting jealous? Let me log off of here before you have a fit. So guess what I did today," she said as she joined me on the bed. "I went and got the police report and I called around and no hospitals had any Jane Does. So, that means my mama is still alive."

"Yes, that is a good sign. We have to keep hope alive. Damn! I sound like Mr. James with that 'keep hope alive' shit. Well, I have to let you know that I am taking over Peanut's trap house."

"You're what? What made you want to do a stupid thing like that?"

"Well, I can name a million reasons, but, for starters, you don't have a job, and these bills around here will be due soon. Look at how much money I made tonight. If I keep doing this, I can save up and get us out of these Bricks."

"Boy, how much money is that?"

"I didn't count it. You can count if for me. I am going to take a shower and get this residue off of me."

Chapter 34: *Easy Come, Easy Go*

I was in the shower, thinking about all of that money that I had just made. It was sweet as pie because all I did was hand them junkies a bag of dope, and they gave me money. I got out of the shower, and Kimmy had lined the money up on the dresser. She had separated all the bills.

"So, how much was it?"

"It was thirty-five hundred dollars, and I am scared."

"What are you scared of?"

"I am scared that you are going to get caught up there and go to jail."

"Baby, don't start thinking like that. What's the motto we live by? If we think positive, we will get positive. And if we speak of negative, then negativity will happen. So, quit thinking crazy, and come and walk me to the door."

"What do you mean? Are you leaving me here all night by myself?"

"I have to go back to the trap house and make this money."

"Well, I'm coming with you," she said as she grabbed

her book bag.

"Look. Listen to me. I don't want you over there hanging out with me, while I am selling dope. We're less than four months away from graduation, and we will not risk your chances of becoming a doctor."

"Well, what about you and your future? Are you thinking about your future, or are you just thinking about this fast money?"

"Look at it like this. If I keep making money like this, we can go live at the Twelve at Atlantic Station if we wanted to. That's the type of money that I am making right now. So, I need for you to stay here, and I will be here in the morning, so we can walk to school together."

"Okay, let me give you a big hug because one day you're here, and the next day you're gone."

"There you go with that tongue again. What did I tell you about that? The tongue speaks power, so, from now on, only let good roll off of your tongue."

"Okay, I love you, baby."

She locked up as I headed back to the trap house. As soon as I walked off of the first step, I heard a voice say, "Nigga, you know what this is! Give me that book bag."

I was getting robbed on my girl's doorstep! I didn't even have time to reach for my gun because I felt his pistol at the back of my head.

"What do you want?" I said, thinking that I was glad that the money was in Kimmy's house. I only had about two hundred dollars on me.

"Nigga, I want that chain, and I want everything that's in your pockets, including the lint. And don't make any sudden moves because I will dome call you right here where you motherfucking stand. Do you feel this .357 Magnum at the back of your head? I will squeeze the trigger if your ass so much as sneezes."

Then, I stood there, frozen, having a flash back, thinking about Trevino. I bet he was feeling how I was feeling right then when I had the gun pointed at him. And what made matters worse, the Bricks were pitch black, and I bet no one saw what was going on. Well, maybe a few junkies witnessed this, but they wouldn't come out until it was over. I took my chain off slowly, and then I reached in my pockets and gave him all the money that I had.

"Nigga, empty those back pockets, too. I see these eight hundred dollar jeans that you have on. I know you got some more money somewhere."

I pulled out my school identification card and showed it to him and said, "This is all that I have in my back pockets."

Then, next thing I knew, he was gone, and I turned around and started shooting my pistol in the dark. Then, all of a sudden, I saw people's porch lights coming on. I ran to the trap house and sat on the sofa and thought about what had just happened. I could have been dead if that nigga would have pulled the trigger. That nigga could have knocked me off in a matter of seconds.

Everything happened so fast that my life didn't even blink before my eyes. I was trying to catch on to my voice, but I couldn't. Everything happened so fast. It seemed like it took forever, but it was only a minute or two. I wished that I'd had my pistol in my hand, and then it would have been a gun battle. But that was a lesson learned. I mean, I did have my gun on me, but I just couldn't reach for it. So, from then on, I decided to carry my gun in my hand when I was walking around the Bricks late at night. I always used to wonder what I would do if I ever got robbed. And, when I actually did get robbed, I didn't do shit because that shit was unexpected. But hell! *What robbery is planned?* I wondered. *Only the perpetrator knows when he's about to strike on a nigga.*

I got up and went to the door and served the jays who were lined up like the zombies in Michael Jackson's "Thriller" video. It was after three in the morning, and I had to be at school in a few hours. I couldn't get no sleep because the trap house was booming. But I guess that this was the life of a trap nigga.

Chapter 35: *Twelve*

I got up the next morning and went to Kimmy's. She had already fixed breakfast and had my plate on the table, but I didn't have an appetite. I was too busy thinking about what had happened to me last night. We headed out the door and she said, "Why do you have that gun in your hand?"

I have this gun in my hand because I got robbed last night. And I will not let a nigga get the ups on me again."

"But we're on our way to school, and this is not the Wild Wild West, just because we're on the west wide."

"This is the Wild Wild West, and, if I would have been able to get to my gun, there would have been a chalk outline of a dead body in the street."

"Well, can you put it up because I doubt if anything will happen to us because we're just walking across the street."

"Damn! There goes twelve," I said as I tried to hide the gun under my shirt.

He whipped up on us and jumped out of the car. He looked at me and said, "Correct me if I'm wrong, but I saw what appeared to be a hand gun. I just saw you put it in your britches."

I was caught red-handed, and there wasn't anything that I could do. I couldn't lie my way out of this one. I couldn't run or nothing.

"Do me a favor and put your hands behind your head."

"Are you arresting him?" Kimmy said.

"Yes, I am because of this," he said as he reached and retrieved the gun. "We have enough crime out here in these streets, and it's coming from y'all young ones."

"How long will he be locked up? How much it costs to get him out of jail?"

"I can't answer any of those questions."

Kimmy started to cry as the police officer put me in the back of the squad car.

"I love you," she said as she walked slowly to school with her head down.

He put the gun in a plastic bag and turned his blue lights off. All I could do on that ride to jail was think about Mr. James saying that I was not about this life. He said that I had to deal with the consequences.

We arrived at the police precinct next to Club Crucial on Bankhead. But, when we got there, he didn't get me out of the car right away. He got out of the car and laughed with another officer. I sat in the back uncomfortable with those handcuffs cutting my circulation in my wrists.

"Fuck!" I screamed out loud, thinking that, if my granny found out about this, it would break her heart. She had always told me not to get into any shit, and, now, look at this shit. I was in the back of a police car, about to go down for a damn pistol. I could only hope that it was a legit gun and that it didn't have no bodies on it.

"Fuck!" I screamed again because I was shit out of luck. If it wasn't for that pussy-ass nigga robbing me last night, I wouldn't have been so paranoid today. The cop finally decided to take me inside, so I could get booked in. First, I had to sit in the holding cell for a few hours. It looked like a club in there. Everyone still had on their regular clothes. I sat down and used the free phone call to call Peanut, but he didn't answer. I didn't have anyone else to call. My granny was at Grady, and Priscilla was probably home, too cracked out to answer the phone. So, after I told a few niggas what I was in for, I got some jailhouse lawyer advice. I wanted to tell them, if it was that easy, then why the fuck were your asses locked up, too. I didn't want to hear that shit that they were talking. I wanted to get out of this smelly jail.

One dude had a crowd around him because he was in there free styling a rap, saying "fuck the police". I listened to that bullshit for a while. Then, I heard one of the officers call my name. I had to take off everything, including my blue Ralph Lauren boxers. If your boxers weren't white, you had to be butt ass naked in that orange Fulton County jumpsuit. It was a good thing that I had on a white T-shirt and that they let me keep that on. Because it was cold as hell in there. My granny had always told me to keep on clean underwear, and she told me to always wear a T-shirt under my clothes even in the summertime.

I took a mug shot. Then, I was released to population. I was assigned to a four man cell. I looked around at my cellmates. Two were Mexicans, and one was black.

"Where you from?" the black boy asked me as I walked in.

"I'm from Zone One Bankhead. Where are you from?"

"Oh, okay. That's what's up. I know a few niggas from the West. Do you know Tarr, Scott, or Outlaw? I know Blalock and Tony from Club Space. That nigga Blalock be in there taking pictures and shit. He make everybody that comes in that bitch look like a star. His saying is 'Everybody is a star in Club Space'. But do they really got a spaceship in that motherfucker? I really like Club Space though because it's big as hell, and, when I get drunk, I can just hit the expressway and ride back to the East Side. But I'm from Zone Six. Have you ever heard of Alley Boy, Dre, Trouble, KK, Sosa, Black, B-Green, or Young Dave? Nigga, I know you done heard of Duct Tape Entertainment. I know you heard of that nigga KK. He's always talking about the GD's. But anyway I am from where them niggas are from. I represent Zone Six all day. I know a few niggas from the Southside like Oowee and Goldie. They're from College Park, and they are always putting on in the clubs and shit. And that boy Oowee has knocked a few niggas out cold at that Mexican bar on Old National. But fuck all of that. My black ass is in here on some bullshit. These crackers said that they got me on video surveillance robbing a cracker in Inman Park. I'm not saying shit until I see my lawyer. The district attorney keep coming to me and offering me time. I looked at that cracker and told him that he better get the fuck away from me before I spit in his face. They got the wrong guy. I am not that guy. Anyway, what are you in here for?"

"I am in here for toting a pistol."

"Did it have any bodies on it?"

"I don't know yet."

"You better pray that it don't have not even one body on that bitch because, if it does, then those crackers gon' put every other dead body they can on you. And I know what I'm talking about because I have seen the shit done before.

"I been trying to get in touch with my nigga to let him know that I am going down for one of his pistols, but he hasn't answered."

"Damn! That's fucked up because, if it's clean, then you're good, but, if it's not, then you're fucked."

Chapter 36: *A Slap on the Wrist*

While I was locked up, that Zone Six nigga kept asking me if I knew different niggas. He asked me if I knew the police officers Roger and Roget. He said that they were twins who often worked the Old National strip at those clubs. He would always talk and never shut up. I was tired of hearing that jail house talk.

I had been locked up for three months, and, during that time, no one came to see me, not even Kimmy. I tried calling her a few times, but she don't have collect calls on her phone. I was in jail on my birthday. Now, ain't that some shit. And so far I hadn't gotten a court date. I was just in that bitch, stuck. I didn't want to interact with too many niggas, so I only associated with my cell mate. He was cool, and, every time he talked to someone in there, he let them know that he was from Zone Six. He didn't give a fuck who he talked to, and he had two teardrop tattoos under each eye.

I didn't want to eat that food. It was so nasty. And they only fed it to us twice a day. Some of them would fight over my food when I said that I didn't want it, and that caused friction.

I only drank that nasty-ass flavored water. I was good because I had some money on my book, and I had plenty food from the store. I had heard a lot of stories about jail, and, so far, I was good because I stayed to myself. I wasn't going to get fucked in the ass by a nigga, nor was I going to fuck another nigga in the ass. I listened to some of those niggas who were waiting to go down the road. Some of them had life sentences, and some of them had ten to thirty years. I sat there and listened to the crimes that they had committed, and some of them just didn't give a fuck. One man said that he don't regret shit that he had done. He said that somebody had robbed him, and he found out who it was. He said that he let the situation die down for a minute. Then, he made his move and killed the nigga who robbed him.

"That nigga tied me up, and he tied my baby mama up, and he even tied my kids up. His ass had to die. But if it was me doing a lick like that I would have killed everybody in the house, kids and all. That just goes to show how these young niggas jump in the game head first." Then he looked at me and said, "You look like a cool-ass, young nigga. I've been watching you in here and, it's a good thing that you stay to yourself. Don't tell none of these niggas your business because they will use it against you in the long run. I am going to be in prison for the rest of my life. I will never be able to see my family again. But I am a real G, one of the few original gangsters left. I wouldn't be a G if I didn't kill that nigga for what he did. I listen to this rap music that these niggas are rapping today, and I have lived that shit. There are a lot of studio gangsters out there. But you look like a good kid. You're quiet, which means you're an observer. And that's good. You don't do too much talking. You think a lot, and that will take you a long way in life.

So as for me I guess this is my deck of cards that God had laid out for me to play. And some niggas go to jail and turn all Muslim and shit. I don't got nothing against that religion, but I was raised praising Jesus Christ, and I will die praising Jesus Christ. It's a good thing that I have a loyal girl, though. She brings my kids to see me once a week."

I had a lot of respect for him because he stood his ground, but was it really worth him losing his freedom forever? At least, no one got killed in his house. But I guess that that G shit was for real with some niggas.

I was laying on my bunk when a correctional officer came to take me to court. I was looking like a convict, too, because my hair had grown out, and I was looking like a wolf man in the face. My face was covered with my thick black hair. He shackled me at my hands and at my feet and had the nerve to tell me to keep up with him. I was trying to, but the faster I walked the tighter the shackles got around my ankles. When I got to the courtroom, I had to stand up because it was so crowded. Then, finally, after a few hours, I was called to stand before the judge. The judge gave me five years probation because this was my first time getting in any trouble and because the gun didn't have any bodies on it after all. He gave me time served, and I was able to get out of jail. As soon as I got back to my cell, my name was called again. I was thinking, *What the hell do they want with me now? Did the judge change his mind and decide to give me some time after all?*

"Demetrius, you have a visitor."

When I got to the visiting room, I thought I was going to see Kimmy or Peanut, but it was neither one of them. It was my granny. I picked up the phone, and, before I could say anything, she started talking.

"Son, how are you doing? Have they touched you in there? Son, didn't I tell you not to get in any trouble?"

"Granny, I am good, and this is a lesson learned for me. When did you get out of the hospital?"

"I got out last week, and I am doing good, too. The doctor told me that I have to cook healthy foods now. I am glad that your uncle is in rehab, and I put Priscilla out of my house. It tore me to the bottom of my heart to do it, but she don't want to change. And I have watched her smoke that crack rock shit half of her life. I never knew that a child of mine would turn out like that. Priscilla was so smart coming up. But then she let those drugs get a hold of her, and now it's like she's a whole different person. Demetrius, when you get out of here, you stay away from that damn Peanut. I told you that he's nothing but trouble. I'll be damned if I let these streets have you. But I do have some good news, though. When I was in the hospital, I found your cousin. And I know that God is working it out. God couldn't have showed up and showed out at a better time. He gave me my health back, and he gave me my other grandson."

"But I thought I was the only grandson. Are you saying that I have a brother somewhere?"

"No, I am saying that your Uncle Red has a son. But the woman he had him by was so crazy that she didn't let him see him. So while I was at the hospital, the security guard was passing out fliers with a picture of a young boy on it. The flier read 'Do you know this boy?' And I knew him from anywhere because he looks just like your Uncle Red did when he was a boy. This is the flier of your cousin."

I looked at the flier, and I almost choked because it was Trevino on the flier.

Chapter 37: *Family Matters*

I was in a zone as my granny went on and on about how she knew that that was her other grandson. She held the flier up and said, "How could someone shoot him in the head and leave him for dead? He has been in the hospital for almost six months now. He has a brain injury because the bullet pierced the left side of his brain."

On the day that she was being released, she got the flier of a John Doe that was admitted to Grady. She was so happy that she had found her other grandson, but I was at a loss for words. I couldn't tell her that I was the one who had shot him and left him for dead. I knew that night that I had seen him move. Granny told me that he had wondered to the KFC on Bankhead, bleeding from the head. She said that someone had seen him and called the police and that he'd been in the hospital ever since.

I had got time served, and I was waiting for my papers to be processed. Granny had left and told me that she was going back to the hospital to sit with Trevino. She said that she wanted to be there when he finally opened his eyes from the coma that he was in. But I couldn't understand for the life of me why Uncle Red never said anything about having a son. But even if he did mention him, I wouldn't have known how he looked. Now that I think about it, he and Uncle Red did have the same eyes.

The next morning, my paperwork came, and Zone Six told me that he would see me when he get out. He said that he had one more question to ask me. And he asked me if I knew a nigga named Juwan who ran with another nigga named Dro. I told him that I didn't know all of those niggas that he kept naming, so we exchanged phone numbers. I walked out of the jail, and the sun was beaming so bright. I walked past Club Crucial, and I saw a white Dodge Charger on the side of the road. It was that street author Antoinette.

"How are you doing?" I asked as I crossed the street.

"I am doing good, and I remember you," she said as she was paying Jake the Tow Man.

Then, she looked at Jake the Tow Man and said that she was so glad that he came to her rescue. She said that her gas hand didn't work and she had run out of gas. So she said she called Jake the Tow Man, and he brought her some gas. She asked me if I needed a ride. Then, she looked at the brown bag that was in my hand and said, "Are you just getting out of jail or something? Get in. I will take you home." We got in her car, and she said, "Strap up. I don't need any tickets. What did you do to go to jail?"

I didn't want to tell her the real reason, so I said, "I was at the wrong place at the wrong time."

Then, she went on about how her son had been in trouble, too. She said that her son Z3 had to learn the hard way. But she said that he graduated from high school, and that he was now focused on his music career. She said that I really reminded her of him. I wanted to interrupt her and tell her that

Kimmy wanted to meet her, but she talked so much about her five kids. She even told me that her friend Cheyvonne was doing hard time in Alto, Georgia because she was at the wrong at the wrong place at the wrong time. She even said that her brother Billy is in jail, too, doing hard time.

Then, she said, "Where do you live anyway?"

I told her that I lived in the Bricks, and she said that she lived in the hood, too, once upon a time. She said that she had lived in Conway Court, Chappell Forest, Anderson Park, Lakewood Village, and Englewood. And she told me the same shit that my teacher had told me: "It's not where you live, it's how you live." She said that she had a child molester for a daddy, and she turned out okay. She even told me that she was adopted and that she had found her real mama at the age of eighteen. Then, I started to wonder if Kimmy's mama had turned up.

Antoinette was talking about some of everything. She was saying how she needed to sell her books and hustle up her bill money. I respected her hustle though because she was a girl out here getting money.

When we pulled up at the Bricks, I saw Peanut's car parked at Kimmy's house. I didn't know what to think. So I told her to drop me off at home. But I couldn't bring myself to go in. I wanted to know why neither one of them came to see me while I was locked up for three months. I knocked on the door very hard, like I was the police. Kimmy came to the door, and she didn't look like herself.

I said, "Are you going to invite me in?"

She had a confused look on her face, and, by that time, Peanut had come to the door, also.

"What's up, Black Boy? I was wondering when those crackers were going to let you out."

"What's going on over here?" I said as I looked around

and saw that the house was dirty. "How come neither one of you came to see me? I thought that you were my girl."

Then, Peanut said, I didn't come because I was trying to see how loyal you were. I wanted see if you would tell them where you got that gun from."

"Well, I didn't say anything. I sat in there waiting for you, and, when I get out, you're over here, chilling with my girl. What's up with that shit? Kimmy, do you have anything to say?"

"I will let you two talk," Peanut said as he left.

Kimmy was kind of distant. Then, she said, "Come here. Let me show you something. Look at this." She pointed at her computer and said that she wanted Keana Balloons to do our wedding.

"What fucking wedding? First, you have to tell me what you're doing in here with that nigga Peanut. And I'm not a fool, so don't play me like one."

"Okay. I will tell you from the beginning. It all started on the day when you got locked up. I was walking to catch the bus to come and see you. But Peanut pulled up, and, for some reason, he knows everything that happens before it happens. He told me that you were going to be in jail for a long time because the gun that you got caught with was stolen. And he said that you would be looking at a maximum of five years. Then, he asked me to take a ride with him. We rode to meet Juan Sanchez. He said something like he was in the Mexican Cartel. So, anyway, he came back to the car, and he had some powdered cocaine. He said that he knew what would keep my mind off of my mother. He told me to take a few bumps off of a one hundred dollar bill that he had rolled up. I didn't know what to do at first, but I was so depressed about my mama, so I did what he said. And it did take my mind off of her for a moment. Then, I needed more, and he fed me more. But, baby,

I promise that I wanted to come and see you. I promise that I still love you. I can bounce back. It's not that bad."

"Did you fuck that nigga?" I said as I punched a hole in the kitchen wall. She started to cry.

"What the fuck are you crying for? You just told me all of that shit and you expect me to be happy. Look at this place and look at you. You don't even look like yourself. And is that the same hair in your head that I got done three months ago? Have you looked at yourself in the mirror lately? I can't believe that you let that nigga trick you like that. I thought that you said that you loved me."

"Baby, I do love you."

"You don't love me because, if you did, you would have came to see me. I was in jail for my birthday, and I didn't even receive a birthday card or nothing. But you never told me that you loved me. So you think that that nigga Peanut loves you? I even told him to stop disrespecting you by calling girls out of their name in front of you. And you fell for that weak-ass game that he fed you. Whatever happened to you praying? Baby, you are so much smarter than that. You, out of all people, know how drugs destroy the body, and, not only did you try it once, you have been doing it for three months! Now, I am going to ask you one more time — did you fuck that nigga?"

I had so much anger in me, and I didn't know what I was going to do if she said that she fucked him. Her pussy was so good to me, and the thought of her fucking Peanut, or any other nigga for that matter… I don't think that I could handle something like that.

"What's taking you so fucking long to answer the question?"

"Why are you cursing at me?" she said as she tried to hold my hand. "If I tell you the truth, will you still be with me?"

My heart sank in my chest because I had a feeling that she was about to tell me that she fucked him.

"I am going to tell you the truth because I love you. Yes, we did have sex, but—"

"But what?"

"But it didn't mean anything."

That was it. I sprinted across the street to Peanut's trap house, and Kimmy followed me. He was serving a few junkies at the door, but, when they saw how pissed I was, they moved out of my way. And before Peanut could say anything, I grabbed him and threw him down the steps. He was a tall, skinny, lanky nigga, so I threw his ass around like a rag doll. He didn't have a chance. I thought about all of the shit that Kimmy had said. I thought about Trevino, and, if it wasn't for him, he wouldn't be almost brain dead. He was trying to talk, but he was too geeked up to speak. By the time I was done with him, he couldn't move. I was kicking his ass like Ice T kicked Nino Brown's ass in New Jack City. I kicked him one last time in his face and said, "You're a pussy-ass nigga with a mouth full of gold."

Chapter 38: *Granny*

While I was stomping the shit out of Peanut, I had a flashback of when I was wailing on Uncle Red's head. There was no stopping me. Peanut had taken me under his wing, showed me the lavish life. Then, he fucked my girl and got her hooked on drugs when I got locked up. As I continued to beat the shit out of him, I only saw red, and it was his blood that was pouring from his face. Then, all of a sudden, I heard my granny's voice, and I had to stop.

"Demetrius, that's enough," she said as she grabbed me off of him.

Even though the whole neighborhood had egged me on to finish the job. I couldn't because I didn't want to be the reason that my granny had a heart attack or another stroke. I kicked him one last time and said, "Nigga, you will respect me or else."

Kimmy followed us home, and she was crying because she knew that I had just beat the living shit out of Peanut because of her.

Granny said, "I don't know what that foolishness was

about, and I don't want to know but, from now on, you're going to leave all this mess behind you. I will not lose you to these streets. You're going to graduate and make something out of yourself. And why didn't you tell me about Coach Breylan's boxing camp? That will be good for you. You have a lot of frustration built up in you, and boxing is a good way to release some of that pain and anger. Demetrius, you will do one or two things while you're living under my roof. You will further your education by going to a trade school. Or you will get a job. It's just that simple."

As we were about to walk in our house, I told Kimmy that I needed some space. I told her that I didn't feel like seeing her right now. And my granny stepped in and said, "Demetrius, let her in. I'm sure, whatever you two are going through, you can get through it together."

This really didn't concern my granny, but she knew best. I wondered, if I had told her that Kimmy was on drugs and that she'd fucked Peanut, if she would she still want her to come in then?

"You two have been friends too long to stop being friends now. You all were raised in the church together, so don't let the devil take y'all friendship away. The devil is real, and he comes to kill, steal and destroy."

As my granny continued to talk and make me feel sorry for Kimmy, I noticed how thin she'd gotten since she had the stroke. Her skin complexion had lightened up, but her hair had turned white as snow. We all sat in the living room, and Kimmy looked so pitiful. My heart felt sorry for her. I felt sorry for her because her mama was still missing, but that shouldn't have been a reason for her to fuck my homeboy. Then, my granny stretched her recliner back and looked at Kimmy and said that she was sorry that her mother hadn't turned up.

"Just keep praying, baby, and the good Lord above will

bring her home."

I knew that my granny was about to preach a sermon. And even though I didn't want to listen, I had to because she only wanted the best for me. She looked at me and said that she had some excellent news.

"Demetrius, we are finally getting Section 8. I have been on that waiting list ever since you were a baby. And it finally came through. We can move into a house and not have to worry about drive-bys. Your cousin Trevino will come and live with us. The doctors said he's doing a lot better, and I said that's because I have been praying. But he will need someone by his side twenty-four/seven because he has to be fed and he has to wear a pamper. This will be a huge surprise for Uncle Red, but he will be saddened at the circumstances. I still can't believe someone would do him like that. It's funny how things happen in life. I had a stroke and found my other grandson in the process. God is good all the time. Can you believe that they were going to pull the plug on him because no one came forward? They said that he will need around the clock care because his brain isn't functioning properly. They said that he'd probably be a vegetable if he did pull through. But I told those doctors that he has a praying grandmother and he will pull through this. I had to let that doctor know that the God I serve will not let that happen."

I listened to my granny go on and on about Trevino, and the guilt was killing me because I was the one who had shot him. Then, all of the "what if" questions started popping in my head. What if I had let Trevino kill Peanut? What if I had spent the night with Kimmy that night? But what if my granny wouldn't have had that stroke? Then, Trevino would have died anyway. She said that they were going to pull the plug on him. Now, I had to figure out how in the hell I was going to tell granny that I was the one who had shot Trevino.

Chapter 39: *Trevino*

I had thought about Trevino so much that I had nightmares about him. I was very hesitant about telling Granny or Uncle Red that I had shot him. But Granny had always said that the truth shall set you free. Kimmy had moved in with us in our apartment. We both were excited about graduation, and I was glad that we were going to move into a house. I had lived in these Bricks all of my life and so had Kimmy. I had to take extra classes since I had missed three months of school. But I pulled my grades up, and I was ready to graduate, too. I told Mr. James that I might consider going to Coach Breylan's boxing camp. I didn't see much of Peanut, but there was a rumor going around that he was going to kill me. But that didn't stop me from walking back and forth to school.

While I was at school, no one said anything to me because they knew that I didn't take any shit. So the word had got back to the school that I had beat up the hood's most influential nigga. Some of the kids couldn't believe it. Even Lenny wanted to be cool with me, but that was strange, considering we used to fight all the time. We, eventually, became good friends, and I even found out that his mama was a crack head, too. So, we had a lot in common.

The time was about to come for Trevino to be released from the hospital. Granny was so happy, but I didn't know how to feel. I wondered, if he got his memory back, would he know that it was me who had shot him? I started to feel bad because I was the reason he was in the situation that he was in.

Granny cleaned the house very good, so there would be no germs. Granny opened the windows, so the strong bleach smell would clear out some. She was so excited about her other grandson coming home. Then, she said that she wished that Priscilla would get her act together. But that would be a cold day in hell because she was so gone off of that crack. We heard a horn blow, and it was the ambulance bringing Trevino home. Granny opened up the door and waved her hand to let them know that they were at the right address. I had butterflies in my stomach. For some reason, I didn't want to face him.

"Come on out here and help me get your cousin," Granny said as she walked out the door. The closer I got to the ambulance, the more my heart raced. They pulled him out on the stretcher, and his eyes were closed. Everyone looked at us as this was happening. They were so nosy and wanted to know what was going on. They brought him in the house, and they laid him in my bed. Granny told me that I had to sleep on my floor, so I could have access to him. I looked at him and saw that the right side of his head was shaved, and he had a deep scar. I held his hand and started to cry. And then I was thinking that, if his mama would have only let Uncle Red see him, we would have been close. But the damage was already done, and I didn't know how to undo something like this. He had tubes in his nose and IV's in his arm.

"What the fuck have I done?" I said as tears continued to roll down my face. Then, I began to pray out loud. I said,

"God, please let him pull through. God, he didn't deserve this and please let him forgive me. And most importantly, God, can you please forgive me? I didn't know that he was my cousin. And now look at him. He's all fucked up because of me."

I looked at the pamper that he was wearing under the hospital gown that he had on. He would never get to have kids or even have sex. He looked like a malnourished kid, and it was all my fault. The feeling was so overwhelming that I didn't know what else to do. All I could do was cry.

I couldn't control the tears that fell down my face. Then, Kimmy walked in and said, "Why are you crying? You don't even know him."

"I am crying because I feel sorry for him. I am crying because my mama is on crack. I am crying because your mama is still missing. I am crying because real niggas cry, too."

Granny walked in and said, "Look at him. He looks just like Uncle Red."

Then, she looked at me and said, "Son, it's going to be alright. I had a dream last night, and God assured me that everything is going to be alright. This is just an obstacle that God put before us, so we can become a stronger family. He's doing good though because he has opened his eyes, but he cries a lot because he wants to get up."

Then, she showed me how to feed him.

"We have to feed him through this tube in his stomach until he's strong enough to eat on his own."

She pulled up his shirt and I almost threw up. I saw a bag on him that was full of piss and shit.

Then, I said, "Why does he have to wear a bag and a pamper?"

She explained that his bowels were reversed, and that it was a good sign because soon he would be off the bag.

Then, Granny said that she found us a four bedroom

house with two and a half bathrooms on the East Side. She said that I would have my own room again once we got settled. She even said that Priscilla could come back and live with us because life was too short. I was listening to her, but I was still in a zone, thinking about Trevino. I couldn't believe that that bullet had done so much damage. And I had to build my nerves up to tell her that I was the bad guy. I had to tell her that it was me who had left Trevino for dead.

Chapter 40: *Nothing but the Truth*

The first few months were not easy when Trevino came home. He cried a lot, and he used to holler in his sleep. And when he was awake, he would just stare at us. But my granny said that was normal because he had sustained a brain injury. She said that Trevino felt love because he had cracked a few smiles at her. Kimmy and I graduated with honors, and my granny was so proud of me. It was almost time for us to move to our new home. The summer was approaching, and it felt good to leave the Bricks once and for all.

Granny and I had packed all of our clothes. And we had bombed the house the day before. Granny said that she would not be taking any roaches with us to our new house. Granny told me to roll Trevino outside, so he could get some air. He had been in the house since he came home, and, since his health was improving, she wanted him to see some sunshine. I helped him into his wheelchair, and he held onto me very tight. He just looked at me and smiled. He couldn't say shit.

All he could do was make noises and point at things. He would slobber, and my granny kept a bibb around his neck. It was like he was a baby all over again. He was almost eighteen, but he was like a kid because he was so helpless.

We were sitting on the porch, and all of the kids crowded around him. I put one of my fitted caps on his head, so that they wouldn't see the cut in his head. The tubes had been removed, and he was now breathing on his own, but he had yet to gain his speech back. My granny said that, once his brain healed, he would be able to speak again. But she said that would be a miracle because the bullet was still lodged in his brain. But she said that we would have to teach him everything that he had learned all over again. She said that we would have to teach him colors, counting, and even how to walk again. She said that basically everything that he knew would have to be learned again. Granny said that she wouldn't mind raising him all over again. Granny told the kids not to get too close to Trevino. I mean, they were looking at him like he was a circus act. I had gotten used to the way he looked, but I was still feeling guilty. I mean, when I changed his pamper, he just looked at me like he knew something. But he didn't. The doctors told granny that it would be a miracle if he'd remembered anything.

As the sun began to set, Granny told us to get in the house. Then, a car pulled up, and no one got out. I didn't recognize the car, so I hurried up and wheeled Trevino in the house. Since I hadn't seen Peanut, I didn't know what that fool was up, too. But I didn't want to take any chances, so I locked up and rolled Trevino in the living room. He liked to watch cartoons, and I sat there and watched them with him. He would point at the television and laugh. But I think that he was amused with the bright colors.

Kimmy was in the kitchen helping Granny cook. Granny didn't cook soul food anymore. She cooked healthier food. She didn't even have to take high blood pressure medicine because she knew how to prepare her food with no salt. I heard a knock at our door, and I looked out of the peep hole. There were two men in suits. And then I heard one say as they continued to knock, "Open up. This is Detective Scott from Fulton County Police Department."

I opened the door, and they held up their badges.

"Are you Demetrius Terrell Smith, also known as Black?"

"Yes, he is," my granny said as she walked in drying her hands. "And who are you?" Granny said as she invited them in, closing the door.

"Well, I am Detective Scott, and this is my partner Detective Turner. We have reason to believe that Demetrius here was involved in a shooting that took place last year."

When he said that, my heart dropped. My granny looked at them and said, "There must be some type of mix up because my grandson doesn't mess around with guns."

Then, one of the detectives opened up a brown paper bag and said, "Are these your clothes?"

He pulled out the clothes that I'd had on the night I shot Trevino. They were still covered in dried up blood.

Granny looked at me and said, "Demetrius, what is going on?"

I looked at Trevino and said, "Granny, I was going to tell you, but I didn't know how."

"Tell me what, son? And why are these clothes covered in blood? And you can't deny those clothes because I bought them."

It seemed like everyone had gotten quiet all of a sudden. I felt like I was on trial for murder. It was so quiet in there, and I felt so nervous. I didn't want to go to jail for the rest of my life for attempted murder.

"Son, what have you done?"

I looked at my granny, and I began to speak. But my words were coming out twisted and a bit confused.

"It all started when I was leaving Kimmy's house one night, and I saw Peanut getting robbed. So, I rushed the boy who had the gun on Peanut. Peanut made me get in the back seat of his car and hold a gun on the boy. And Peanut had passed me the blunt, but I choked on it because I had never smoked weed before. And then the boy tried to take the gun from me, and it accidentally went off. It was a mistake, Granny. I swear that I didn't mean to do it. I am telling you nothing but the truth."

"Son, what are you trying to say?"

"Granny, I am saying that it was me who shot Trevino and left him for dead."

Chapter 41: *Leaving the Bricks*

While I continued to pour my heart out, Kimmy sat there with her mouth wide open.

"Oh, my God!" Granny said as she looked over at Trevino. "You mean to tell me that it was you who did this to him?"

"Yes, Granny. It was me, but it was a mistake."

"I heard you when you said that the first time. But he's a human being. How come y'all didn't take him to Grady?"

"Peanut had said that he was dead, and he said that, if the gun wouldn't have went off, he would have shot him himself."

Then, my granny looked at the detectives and said, "So, what's going to happen now?"

One of them said that, since we left him for dead, I had to answer to that. And the other one said that Trevino would have to press charges for me to go to jail. And considering his situation, he wouldn't be able to because his mother was dead and we were his next of kin. Then, we heard a knock at the door. Kimmy went to the door, and it was Uncle Red. He walked in on us in the living room and sat on the sofa. Granny hugged him and said that he came back home just in time. Then, Uncle Red looked over at Trevino in the wheelchair and said, "Who is that? What's going on, Mama?"

Granny started to tear up as she looked at Trevino and said, "First, I want to say that I love you, and you look good and healthy. That is your son Trevino over there in that wheelchair, and Demetrius shot him."

Uncle Red walked over to Trevino, and he didn't even know what was going on. Then, I started explaining myself again. I tried to explain to Uncle Red that it was an accident. But he just cried as he hugged Trevino and told him that he was so sorry for not being there for him. It was like a family reunion all over again. Uncle Red hadn't seen his son since he was a baby. And now when he did finally see him again he had a bullet lodged in his head. I knew that he was mad at me, and I could tell because a vein popped up in the middle of his forehead. And that vein would always come in his head when he was mad.

My granny said, "Now, son. Don't go to blaming yourself. It was Veronica who didn't let you see him. Red, everything happens for a reason."

"Mama, I don't want to hear that. Now is not the time. What reason did this happen for? My son gets shot by my nephew, his own cousin."

"Well, you look good, son, and I am glad that you went to rehab. But Trevino will pull through, I know this because God has done some miraculous things for this family. He brought me back from a stroke, and he got you sober from alcohol, and now he is bringing Trevino back from being brain dead. And it's only a matter of time until he fixes that daughter of mine, too."

The detectives told Granny that the district attorney

would be contacting her soon. They left, and Granny looked at me and said, "Son, we all make mistakes, but this is one that you should have spoken up about. But I won't play the blame game either. I just hope that you don't have to go to jail behind this."

Then, I started to think that, if I had to go back to jail, I would have to listen to those same flexing-ass niggas. Like that nigga who had talked my ear off from Zone Six. He swore he knew everybody from Techwood Ced all the way to Chubb in Savannah. Then, I thought about how Peanut had played me and said that he had burned my clothes. I knew I should have gotten them when I had the chance. He couldn't take that ass whipping, so now he was going to extreme measures to get me locked up.

The tension settled down in the room, and I had to give it to Uncle Red. He looked like a whole new person. Granny told Uncle Red the good news about her getting Section 8. She said that he came home just in time, so he could help the movers, but Uncle Red just had a dazed look on his face.

"Mama, you know all my life all I ever wanted was to be in my son's life and now look at him."

"I know, son, but, trust me, we will be alright."

Kimmy and I went in my room, and I knew that I was going to hear her mouth, too.

"So, that was the gangster shit that Peanut was saying that you did? I am at a loss for words, but people always say what they would do and they don't know what they would really do unless they're put in that position. I understand what you had to do, but— Damn! —he could have died."

"But he didn't die, and I don't need this from you right now!"

"I'm sorry," she said as she closed the door.

She looked around the room and saw all of the Trevino's

things lined up on the dresser.

"I hope he pulls through," she said as she hugged me.

"I hope he does, too."

It was time for us to move to our new home. And we were on our last trip. Uncle Red was at our new house with Trevino. So it was my granny, Kimmy, and me still moving the last of our things. It was getting dark, and Granny was saying that she was glad that she was finally leaving the Bricks. Then, all of a sudden, we heard something that sounded like firecrackers. But then it got louder and louder and closer to us. I noticed what was going on first. It was a drive by. I saw Peanut hanging out of the window of a white Crown Victoria holding a Tech Nine. I ran as fast as I could when I noticed that I wasn't hit. When the coast was clear, I saw that Kimmy and my granny weren't so lucky. I walked over to Kimmy, and she had blood coming from her head and chest.

"Get up!" I yelled. "Can you hear me, Kimmy? Please get up! I love you!"

But there was no life left in her body.

"I never got the chance to tell you that I love you. Baby, please! Get up! It's me! Demetrius!"

I kept holding her, crying, rocking back and forth.

Then, I heard my granny grasping for air. She'd been shot in the back. Her eyes were wide open, and she wasn't moving. She was laying on her stomach, and she was breathing very heavy. And I tried to wake her up. I was crying and saying, "Granny, please wake up! Granny, can you hear me? Please wake up! It's me! Demetrius! I love you, Granny. Please don't leave me like this."

Chapter 42: *A New Me*

When the ambulance had got there, they put Kimmy in a body bag and put my granny on a stretcher. They took her to Grady, and she was in critical condition. I was glad that she didn't die. I grabbed my strap, and I went to the trap house looking for Peanut, but he was gone. I didn't care who saw me with my gun in my hand. I stayed at the bottom of his steps and waited for him to come back, but he never showed up.

Uncle Red and I took turns going to visit my granny. When he went to see her at Grady, I had to stay at home with Trevino. And when I wanted to go visit her, he stayed at home with Trevino.

Despite what happened, we were still family. And, for the most part, we had to get along. We lived together, and Granny wouldn't have wanted it any other way. My granny was still in critical condition, and it wasn't looking too good for her. I stayed by her side, and I prayed for her day in and day out. But her condition worsened, and she eventually passed away during surgery.

We had her funeral at Donald Trimble Funeral Home,

and it seemed like the whole west side was there. Everyone respected my granny because she was so good to everyone who she came in contact with. Priscilla even showed up, and she said that she was off of drugs, but I knew better because she was high at the funeral. I had lost my girl and my granny in the blink of an eye. I was glad that Granny had changed her insurance policy and put my name on it. Because Priscilla would have smoked it up. I really wanted her to change like Uncle Red, but she didn't.

She came by the house from time to time to eat and bathe, but that was about it. She never was a mama to me, so I didn't miss her. I missed my granny, and I cried every night like a baby because I knew that once I saw her in that casket that there was no coming back.

Uncle Red and I often talked about the good old days. He told me that he forgave me for what I did. He said that he understood that shit happens. He blamed his ex wife for not letting him see Trevino. He said that, if she would have let him see Trevino, he wouldn't have turned to alcohol. And he said that Trevino wouldn't have joined any gangs. I felt sorry for him because of the way in which he had finally reunited with his son. Trevino never did learn to talk. All he did was stare at us and smile.

My granny was buried at Lincoln Cemetery, and so was Kimmy. I visited them every day. I had got my driver's license, and I had bought myself an '86 Oldsmobile Cutlass Supreme. The district attorney had dropped all the charges that were against me. And I was relieved because I had been through so much in these past few months. I wished Kimmy was alive to see that Curtis was charged with her mother's murder. They had found her car in Loganville, and she was dead in the trunk. Curtis had confessed to her murder, and he, also, said that he was the one who had robbed me, but I knew that Kimmy was now in heaven with her mama and my granny.

Peanut was serving life for killing my granny and Kimmy. And I was glad for his ass because he needed to be somebody's bitch in prison. I didn't hang in the streets anymore. I just took life one day at a time. I was more patient than I used to be. And I learned to be very humble. Especially since I lost my granny.

If I even thought about doing something bad, her voice would pop in my head. I went to Coach Breylan's boxing camp, and I started my own mentoring program. Coach Breylan knew a lot of people, and he helped me get a contract with the Boys and Girls Club of Atlanta. I was a counselor, and Mr. James was so proud of me, and I was glad that he never gave up on me. I was glad to help the kids of our future. And when I told them my story, they were all ears. And I knew in my heart that my granny was looking down and smiling at me.

I never thought in a million years that I would lose my granny to violence. As much as she preached about not wanting to lose me to the streets, I ended up losing her to the damn streets. She told me to not ever question God, but I wanted to ask Him, why did He take my granny like that? Why didn't he take me instead?

About The Author

Antoinette Tunique Smith was born in San Francisco, California and raised in ATL, where she still resides. She is blessed with five children who are known as the five lights of her life: Pinky, Driah, Clyde, Chicken and Fat Boy.

She would like people to know that it doesn't matter where you come from, you can be whatever you wanna be. Just believe in God. There is a God!

Thanks & Much
respect,
Antoinette Smith

AND PLEASE CHECK OUT ANTOINETTE'S
PREVIOUSLY RELEASED BOOKS:

DADDY'S FAVORITE POP
MARRIED: SNEAKY BLACK WOMAN
WHITE COP, LIL' BLACK GURL
I'M A DRAG, NOT A FAG

AND PLEASE STAY TUNED FOR ANTOINETTE'S UPCOMING
BOOKS:
WOMEN R DOGS TOO!
I'M BI WHY LIE?
TREY AND HIS DNA (SEQUEL TO *I'M A DRAG, NOT A FAG*)
I WISH I WAS RAISED (MY LIFE'S STORY)
MY FATHER'S SEED (SEQUEL TO *DADDY'S FAVORITE POP*)
MARRIED, SNEAKY BLACK MAN (SEQUEL TO *MARRIED, SNEAKY*
BLACK WOMAN)

I really hope you guys enjoy my Straight to the Point Books!!

Reader Comments

Stacey Mobley-Cook – Tampa, Fl. - 3/19/13
I had the pleasure of reading Im a Drag Not A Fag and White Cop Little Black Girl. I truly enjoyed both books.They are well written, grabs your attention from begining to end. I just purchased Married Sneaky Black Woman and Daddy's Favorite Pop I'm sure that I will enjoy them both Keep up the good work

Natasha Parker – United States. - 3/13/13
Please Check this author out..any of Antoinette Smith Books will blow ya mind..It's hard to put the book down becus the stories gets straight to the point!!

Lashonda Jeffries – Atlanta, Ga. - 3/11/13
I love all your books friend. In married sneaky black women i called u a million times wondering how you come up with this stuff. You motive me to the fullest . Love you keep it going

Shacoria Tukes – College Park, GA. - 3/10/13
I must say I didn't like reading at first. My mom told me to read the 1st page of DADDY'S FAVORITE POP...OMG I couldn't put it down! OUTSTANDING, I take my hat off to you. I have read all four of your books. Now I'm waiting on BLACK OUT ON BANKHEAD!

Angela Tukes – Georgia. - 3/10/13
I am a true reader, and must say that you did that, AWESOME! Every book from the 1st to your latest. Keep them coming MAMI. You are a beautiful talented BLACK WOMAN! I know I'm not the only one waiting on a movie...TYLER PERRY WHERE YOU AT!!

Melinda 'Pooh' Pressley – Riverdale, Ga. - 3/07/13

I had the pleasure of meeting Antoinette years before she wrote these books and she told myself and my family her story. And her story inspired her to write 'Daddy's Favorite Pop'. When I read that book I could not put that book down. I rode to Alabama one day and read the entire book and called her with question and asked when the next book comes out. Then here comes 'Married Sneaky Black Woman' it was like a mystery I couldn't go to sleep until I finished reading the damn book. I called her and said "damn u clever as hell" when the next book come out! Then she put out ' White Cop, Lil Black Gurl' man on man.... That was good... I called her up and said next. She put out I'm a Drag not a Fag' this book was so unique. People I am Antoinette Smith #1 fan with the hood books. If she don't hurry up with Black-Out on Bankhead Imma screammmmm!!! Antoinette I love you and keep up the good work. I will see you in the big legend soon!

(DIVA) Michelle Powell – Stone Mountain, Ga. - 2/26/13

I have read Daddy's Favorite Pop.. That was my Favorite that book made me want to read more..Then I read Married Sneaky Black Woman..That book was very Interesting I cant wait to read Pt. 2.. I also read White Cop Little Black Girl.. I don't thin I could have done time I liked that one too. I've read I'm a DRAG Not A Fag..OMG Now that book there I couldn't put It down I went on a Weekend vacation and I read this book two days.. I'm waiting on pt. 2 of Daddy's Favorite Pop.. Just to let you know Antoinette I (DIVA) Am your # 1 Fan I Intend to purchase all of your books as they come out I want the whole Collection. Your are the best writer in my book..Keep them coming PEACE AND LOVE DIVA

TaShanna Word – Journey - 10/23/12

Amazing......You are truly gifted and blessed. I did not put your book down Daddy's Favorite Pop. Can't wait to read the others. I've worked in the social service field for over 15 yrs. I have heard and seen some of the worst cases in my career. Ms. Smith, I would love to have lunch and see if you are able to speak with the teens that are on my case load. Survivor you are and your Future get ready for it ....

Ed Weathers – College Park, Ga. - 8/27/12
I love your books because they talk about real every day people, people you may see on the train or the street and also you help people get there voice out there no matter what.

Sharon LadeeStorem Acres – Atlanta, Ga. - 8/04/12
My name is Sharon {Ladee Storem} Acres and I met you at Big Daddy's soul food place off of Riverdale a few years back and you gave me your card. I have a Radio Show call Claim Your Fame Radio Show on WAEC Love 860 AM in Atlanta Ga and we reach 5 to 6 million listeners, I would love for you to be on the show. My website is www.storemandsun.com or call Storem and Sun Ent. at 678-268-7859

Kaliliah– Atlanta, Ga. - 6/26/12
OMG...This author never cease to amaze me! Excellent writer with amazing story lines! "I'm a drag not a fag" is most definitely a must read. I couldn't stop...I had to get to the end! Keep up the good work Antoinette!! You will always have my support!!

Rosey – United States - 4/27/12
KUDOS to you and your hard work and tremendous success! Keep on going girlfriend... you inspire me ;) All the Best ~Rosey

Tarsha Latrice – College Park, Ga. - 4/04/12
I read your first book and loved it!! Just got my copy of the second book and will start reading tonight!! keep doing your thang....I love your hustle!!!

RIP Nikki Bazile-Mathis
August 21, 1979 - April 11, 2012
Gone, but never forgotten...

www.straighttothepointbooks.com
acansing2000@yahoo.com

www.ingramcontent.com/pod-product-compliance
Lightning Source LLC
Chambersburg PA
CBHW071326250626
47159CB00004B/1477